Circle of Love

Can the discovery of an English Civil War secret bring a new beginning—today?

Susan Cornell Bauer

xulon PRESS

Copyright © 2003 by Susan Cornell Bauer

Circle of Love
by Susan Cornell Bauer

Printed in the United States of America

Library of Congress Control Number: 2003091631
ISBN 1-591606-12-8

All rights reserved. No part of this publication may be reproduced or transmitted in any form or by any means without written permission of the publisher.

Unless otherwise indicated, Bible quotations are adapted from *The Holy Bible, an exact reprint in Roman type, page for page, of the Authorized Version [King James], published in the year 1611,* London: Oxford University Press, 1911.

Illustrations by Paula Lawson

Xulon Press
www.XulonPress.com

Xulon Press books are available in bookstores everywhere, and on the Web at www.XulonPress.com.

Dedicated to
my husband of thirty years,
Gary H. Bauer,
whose character and ancestry
inspired this story,
and to our daughters,
Sara Bauer Wolf
and
Claire Bauer,
for the joy they bring to our lives.

Acknowledgements

Just as the birth of a baby or the release of a video production is a team effort, so is the launching of a book. My heartfelt gratitude goes to everyone who helped! Specific thanks go to the following people, to whom I owe much:

Gary Bauer, beloved husband of my youth (and beyond!), who demonstrates valuable lessons in unconditional love, inspires character qualities of heroes in this story, and twenty years ago started teaching me video production. The ancestry of his late mother, Betty Zle' Bauer, led us to the discovery of the book's setting and provided the seeds of truth from which the fictional story grew.

Claire Bauer and Sara Bauer Wolf, our grown daughters, who in years past gave up some "mommy time" and ate haphazard meals, but love and pray for me anyway. They have encouraged the writing process long-term.

W.C. "Duke" and Ruth Cornell, my loving parents, who sparked my joy in reading, introduced me to Jesus, and urged me toward excellence.

Paul Cornell, my scientist brother, whose passion for

history became contagious.

Richard Bauer, my father-in-law, for his ongoing love and help, and my step-mom, Betty Huddleston Bauer, for reading the manuscript and saying, "Yes!"

Ruth V. Hunter, cousin of my husband, who deeply values family heritage and told us where to find the ancestral home.

John M. Kolbert, author and retired from the registrar's office at the University of Keele, Staffordshire, England. He gave Gary and me our first tour of Keele Hall, made the video documentary possible, and prompted the birth of this story by relating true incidents in Keele's past. John also reviewed the manuscript in detail, through the lens of his history studies at Magdalene College, Cambridge, and his life at Keele. (However, as author, I take responsibility for any and all error, including any related to literary license.)

Francoise Becker and Dr. Walt Becker, of La Vie/The Cottage at Coronado Island, for their friendship since seminary, and for support and assistance in reviewing content from the standpoint of psychology and Christian counseling.

Dr. Archibald Hart, author of *The Anxiety Cure*, for additional information on anxiety, adrenalin and stress. Dr. Hart is former Dean of the Graduate School of Psychology at Fuller Theological Seminary, in Pasadena, California.

Stephanie Castillo, long-time friend and Emmy-award-winning documentary producer from Hawaii, for sharing her research on English church bells and the art of change-ringing. (Additional information was gleaned from my visits to the Church of St. John the Baptist at Keele, St. Margaret's twelfth-century timber church at Betley, and the Cotswolds village church at Lechlade.)

Ben Delves, retired Secretary of Friends of the Ancient High House in Stafford, for data on the 400-year-old town-house and true events there during the 1600's.

Librarians of the Garland Public Library, Ridgewood

Acknowledgements

Branch, for obtaining research materials on inter-library loan, especially the Civil War letters of Sir Edmund Verney and his family living at Aylesbury in Buckinghamshire.

Diane Allen Kanagy, friend from childhood, who used to dream up imaginative stories with me for hours.

Bettye Martin McRae, founder of Writers' Ongoing Workshops®, whose regular meetings encouraged the initial writing and provided valuable critique. Prestonwood Christian Writers, now Southwest Christian Writers' Guild, founded by Jan Winebrenner, continued to fuel my enthusiasm to complete the book.

Dr. Charles Dyer, friend, best-selling author, and Vice-President of Academic Affairs at Moody Bible Institute, Chicago, for advice and encouragement along the way.

Dr. Wanda Vassallo, author and speaker, offered critique and prayers for the project, along with her warm friendship.

Lucille Cunningham, life-long friend and retired professor of English in Austin, Texas, who read the manuscript for critique and inspired me further.

Sally Anderson, journalist and church "home team" friend, for proofreading the semi-final draft.

Darlene Quarterman, Belhaven College roommate and missionary to Ukraine, for affirming my efforts and reading the manuscript with enthusiasm.

Nancy Arrington, Lake Ridge Bible Church friend, for believing in this project, plus praying for and encouraging its publication.

Sharon Geiger, award-winning news journalist at KCBI Radio in Arlington, Texas, for her ongoing interest in Alpha Video Productions' mission projects and in the novel's progress.

Sandra Burgess of Staffordshire, England, who gave historical comment on early portions of the manuscript.

Authors John Dwyer, Dr. Sharon Sneed, Dr. Karen Kletzing, Debbie Piper, Robin Hardy, and Brock and Bodie

Circle of Love

Thoene for their insights along the writing journey. Phil Rawley also gave me sound advice.

Karen Kochenburger, Senior Acquisitions Manager of Xulon Press, for her valuable assistance.

Paula Lawson for her illustrations and Bill Wilson for the author photo.

Most of all, the Lord Jesus Christ receives my deepest gratitude for giving me life, forgiving my sins, calming my own struggles with anxiety, and providing peace with God forever. Any talents I possess are gifts from Him.

Susan Bauer
Richardson, Texas
January 1, 2003

Table of Contents

Prologue xiii

Part I: Tracy 17
    University of Keele, 1992

Part II: Honour 63
    Mayfield Manor, 1642

Part III: Anne 183
    University of Keele, 1992

Epilogue 225

About the Author 227

A Personal Word to the Reader 229

Fact and Fiction 231

To Learn More 233

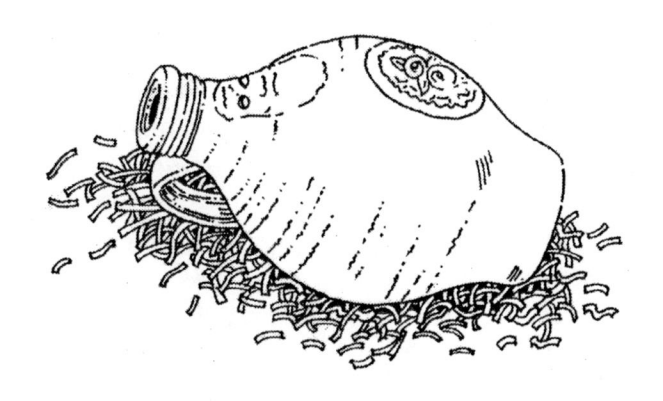

Prologue

Mayfield Manor, Staffordshire, 1642

*T*he simple dairy maid crouched in a cow crib. Her mouth gaped as she watched the secret ceremony unfolding across the barn.

A flickering candle revealed the couple. Their heads bent close. Plumes and sash marked him a soldier of King Charles. Her garments were far more coarse. A lock of the man's long hair brushed the young beauty's neck. He stole a kiss, then caught her round the waist. A band of silver gleamed on her tiny hand.

Candle, pray show faces! urged the lowly observer. *Who meets like this? Her noble bearing ill matches the servant's cap and aproned dress she wears.*

Before the pair, a man of gnarled and shaking hands scratched with quill on parchment. Then with a solemn

Circle of Love

look, he scrolled the paper carefully and entrusted it to the soldier's keeping.

The Cavalier bent for a squat, glazed crock at his feet. Placing the small document within, he took the candle from his beloved, tipped it, and began to seal the opening with tallow.

Before he could finish, the lady caressed his doublet sleeve. The circle of silver caught on a thread and slipped off her finger. It clinked against the ugly crock, then fell muffled into the straw.

"The ring, my love!" The bride fell to her knees in search.

Angry shouts erupted on the path outside. A mighty weight slammed against the barn's wide, oaken doors.

The maid cringed in the hay like a cornered rabbit. *I know that evil voice!* Her eyes darted about the animal stall. *But how shall I escape? Dare I show myself to mine enemy? A hundredfold, nay! To the secret covenant-makers? Again, nay!*

Wood groaned louder. The soldier advanced toward the heaving door bolt. With one hand he balanced the crock and candle; the other rested uneasily on the hilt of his rapier.

"Help! I cannot find it!"

The soldier turned and saw his beloved's stricken face. He kicked straw aside with his boots and bent low with the candle to help her. But the barn door gave yet another mighty heave.

"Come! Shall God grant us life 'til daylight, thy husband will get for thee another." Like a sudden whirlwind, he snapped her up and lunged toward escape.

The aging priest followed, with the witness.

Out went the candle. Feet tangled in the dark. Crockery dropped to the hay and rolled aside. The soldier paused a mere eyelash blink.

"Fear not for the parchment," the old man breathed.

Prologue

"'Ere I sleep this night, the union shall be writ in the parish register."

As wood splintered on the main door, the three made haste through the other portal. The ancient man of the cloth stumbled out last.

Beads of sweat trickled down the dairy maid's forehead.

Only a few feet away, her enemy staggered drunkenly where moments before met the clandestine pair. "Fanny! Fanny!"

Hurling her name through his rotten teeth, the oaf cursed and searched, and cursed again. Then stumbled out the way he came.

She wiped the sweat with a gritty sleeve and crept from hiding on hands and knees. In the darkness, she sifted straw for what the couple left behind.

Even as her fist latched onto the Rhenish ware, greedy fingers searched for more. *Aha!* Heart pounding, she climbed one-handed to the loft and struck flint. A candle from her hidden cache sputtered light.

Treasure beckons. Withdrawing the document, the girl squinted at the marks it bore. *Narry a word can I cipher.*

A gleaming circle rested in her hand. Grubby fingers closed upon it, fairly tasting victuals—and maybe even freedom.

But something gave her pause. *The lift of her head. The whisper of a sacred vow. The pair of gentle hands. So like milady's daughter!* She sighed. *And her the one that salves my wretched wounds when...*

New shouts in the distance ripped her thoughts. As the hoofbeats grew closer, she heard, "Vengeance on the Royalists! Torch and burn! Unseat the tyrant on the throne!"

Biting her lip, the milkmaid thrust her newfound treasure into place. Sloppy candle drippings sealed the opening.

Then she scrambled down the ladder and snatched a shovel.

Circle of Love

By stolen candlelight, the ragged maid lifted chunks of earthen floor. In those cool depths, she secreted the jug, then slipped empty-handed out the doorway into the woods.

Before sunrise, all the outbuildings on that Staffordshire hill lay charred. Yet the low-born chattel had made her choice. A noble choice that kept silence for centuries—but not forever.

Part I: Tracy

Chapter One

∞

Staffordshire, 1992

*T*racy Anne Stevens twisted in the British Rail seat as she saw the destination sign. *I should never have come,* she thought. *Seeing him again will just lead to another goodbye.* Right away, the implications of this gray English Tuesday played havoc with her elegant body.

A tight knot formed in her stomach. Her palms started to sweat. *Not the anxiety again—so soon!* she pleaded. *It's worse than ever since he left. Can't someone release me from this dragon ruining my life?*

The unwelcome rush of adrenalin made her heart pound harder and harder. Heat flashed up her body toward her face.

Tapes of the fearful thoughts began to play in her mind. *I've got to get out of here! Out of here! Away! Away from these people...out into fresh air.*

The feelings of panic that had hounded Tracy since childhood stormed her. They assaulted her carefully controlled image as a worldly-wise, independent woman. All senses focused inward even as her eyes darted toward the vestibule, searching for a way of escape. She rose halfway from the upholstered seat, while another message sought to counter the one echoing insistently in her head.

Her hand clamped vise-like on the chair a row ahead. *You can conquer it, Tracy Anne. Will it to go away. You can conquer it. You can...*

She took several long, deliberate breaths. At last, she managed to force her body back down. The first onslaught paused momentarily.

Tracy pushed back in the coach seat, closed her eyes, and put her carefully manicured fingers against her temples. When the next rush of panic came, she was more prepared for battle. *Again, inhale and exhale. Slow and deep.*

Deliberately visualizing a particular place of beauty, she took herself away to a verdant spreading tree—somewhere in her imagination—where she felt shade, protection and, somehow, love.

There under the fir branches, she experienced slow cleansing of the momentary fright that struck like a vengeful army.

I think I just won a battle. But will the day ever come when the war is over? She felt drained of energy and short on hope.

Again, she looked out the window. The BritRail engine was creeping toward the station.

Her hands shook as she gathered the cashmere coat, Pullman case and carry-on. Tracy swallowed, placed her hand on her nervous stomach, and waited for the train to halt.

It's a good thing I don't get like this before contract-signings with clients, she mused, then caught herself. *Without Fresh Focus Advertising, I don't even have clients to meet with anymore.*

Not since she'd made the mistake of trusting Christopher too little—and Drake too much. Not since her bright new account executive had snowed her on his abilities, his

Part I: Tracy

honesty, and his appeal as a man. Not since Drake Flint had conspired with the preppy little payroll clerk to divert funds into his own account at the bank, cleverly destroying months of past-due notices for Tracy from the Internal Revenue Service. Not since the IRS had padlocked the doors of her creative company two Fridays ago.

How could this happen to me? She went over it again in her mind. *Especially when I've bent over backward to be fair to my clients. So much for the reputation for business integrity I've worked so hard to build!*

It seemed more like a century since she'd lost Fresh Focus, and even longer since Christopher had tired of always being second place in her life.

She sat stiffly as other passengers brushed past her seat, murmuring politely, "Sorry. Sorry." A thin girl about eight years old tripped over Tracy's bag; she softened enough to flash an apologetic smile. The child answered with one of her own.

Tracy couldn't delay any longer. Her legs felt as heavy as her luggage—and her heart—when she finally made her way to the exit.

At the vestibule she paused. *It's not too late. I could go back to London and get a flight home in the morning.*

"Better step off snappy, Miss. The train's departing for Manchester." Another passenger steadied her arm and plopped the Pullman case on the platform pavement.

Tracy made her choice. Shivering in the dreary winter air, she slipped into her coat, took a shaky breath, and stepped off the train. Her hand went to her thick, dark hair right away. It was raining.

As she bent to pull the fur-trimmed hood of her coat around her head, Tracy heard her other name. Then a rush of running feet.

"Anne. Anne!"

Brown eyes met blue for a split second as the man

caught her in a crushing embrace, then drew back quickly. The couple stared at each other.

She searched the expression of this wiry man in his early thirties. A gust of wind caught his ash blond hair and raindrops dotted the sandy beard. His cheeks were ruddier than ever.

Behind rimless glasses, kind blue eyes flicked back and forth, while one hand nervously jangled loose coins in his pants pocket. The bomber jacket he wore had flapped open in his haste.

Why did you invite me here, so out-of-the-blue? she wondered. *Something's going on, something besides just being lonely. When you phoned last week, why did I agree to come at all?*

Behind her, the train to Manchester pulled out of the station.

Unconsciously, she laid her hand against his chest. *He can't have changed much. The miniature screwdriver and flashlight are still there, right in his shirt pocket.* She wasn't thinking rationally anymore.

* * *

He gently pushed back the hood from her thick curls and brushed her cheek with a kiss.

"Christopher," she whispered. Although he couldn't actually hear her greeting, he felt the name against his neck. Like she used to say it.

Christopher Mayfield Montgomery placed his hands on her narrow shoulders and stepped back to gaze once more at her face. The laugh lines around his eyes dared to crinkle in hope. Despite the shadow of past hurts, the light had come back into her eyes. The flecks of amber glowed again. Droplets of rain perched on her eyelashes, or were they something else?

Part I: Tracy

"Anne. Let's begin again." There were tears shining in his eyes.

She blinked but gave no answer.

Chapter Two

Christopher wheeled her suitcase toward the bus stop. Tracy Anne's eyelids felt gritty with jet lag. They drooped closed, then she opened them to glance down the street.

"Look out!" Christopher yelled. He grabbed her free arm and pulled her back to safety, as a Ford Cortina whizzed by. "Look right! Remember where you are?"

"Oh, yeah. Right. Right."

When the lanes cleared, he propelled her across to the bus stop. "My instincts aren't well-trained yet, either, Anne. A lot of things are different here."

He gestured toward the falling rain; a familiar boyish grin spread between his mustaches and beard. "I'm sorry about leaving the umbrella back at the university. You can tell I'm still getting adjusted."

She wrapped her coat tighter but managed a smile. "It's not a bad welcome to the country, really. And, by the way, what do the undergraduates of Keele University think of their video whiz with the Texas twang?"

"Actually, I'm just a guest lecturer in the Communications Department for a semester, teaching about American video production styles." He swept low in a comical bow. "And they're catching on to my distinguished brand of English very well, thank you."

Soon, a red double-decked bus drew up, and the two boarded. Stowing Anne's luggage on the lower level, Christopher motioned her up the tiny stairway. "The view's worth it, I promise."

They found a seat by the front window. From the intimate perch, it was a struggle not to question her, not to assume too much by her mere presence. His whole being remembered what it had been like to be with her, to share himself and his love unreservedly. Since that awful day months ago when he'd moved out, he'd felt only half alive. The other half had been given away, hoping for the commitment that never came.

Am I anything to her? Or has her most recent pain pushed me even farther away? Christopher swallowed those questions once again.

Tracy worked at keeping her eyes on the landscape before her—the church spires and neatly kept brick houses, with their tiny front yards and privet hedges. "All the flowers are dead. It's not like the travel brochures." Her voice was flat. "But the grass is so green."

"I still think it looks like a PBS documentary out there; maybe we're in a magical edit room and the window's the monitor," he teased when they reached a roundabout near the John-O-Gaunt Pub.

"If so, I hope we never finish the project," she murmured.

Mist droplets shimmered then fused and trickled down the bus window, as the winding pavement shined and shop windows glowed in the soft Midlands light.

Tracy Anne, slipping under the influence of jet lag, finally succumbed to Christopher's warmth and the motion of the bus. While she dozed against his shoulder, the curving village road opened out on the rye-green countryside

Part I: Tracy

with its sloping hills and leafy hedgerows. Anne stirred.

She faced Christopher, acutely aware of his firm arm around her tired shoulders. Without a word, he bent closer and gently kissed her lips. His touch was tender. Undemanding. The light brush of his beard felt like home. As the clean scent of him washed over her for the first time in months, her heart unlocked and she responded as a rosebud opens to the summer sun.

"I think it's stopped raining. There's a lovely little inn up ahead. Would you like a bite to eat?"

"That would be nice." Anne nestled closer to his chest.

The bus stopped where the road met a hilltop lane. Christopher steadied Anne to her feet and watched her down the stairs. He retrieved the luggage and they stepped off the bus.

She stared a moment after it departed.

"Something missing?" He surveyed her belongings and immediately tapped his head. "Of course, it's your briefcase. You're never without it." A slow grin emerged. "Could it be you came on this trip just for fun?"

She frowned. "Come off it, Chris. Don't harass me right now."

"You'll feel better after some meat-and-potatoes." He steered her up the short lane toward a low cottage with thatched roof. "Welcome to the Black Horse Inn."

"Why, it's enchanting!"

"The food's great, too, and they always have a cozy fire." Christopher managed the awkward hardware on the inn's thick door. Both he and Tracy Anne had to duck under the beamed doorway. They paused on the stone floor to let their eyes adjust to the dim interior.

He rolled the baggage into a cubbyhole off to the side, then led her toward the welcoming fireplace. They slid into a high-backed alcove facing one another.

"You need some protein to keep you going. That's what

the jet lag diet says, and it worked for me. Like to try some shepherd's pie? It's my favorite."

"That sounds fine, Christopher. Thank you." There was something delicious about the sound of his name on her tongue, and she relished it. But nagging at the back of her mind was that question—*Why did he ask me to come?*

The waitress walked over to the table and looked at Chris.

"Two ginger beers, with lime. And shepherd's pie for each of us." He turned to Tracy. "The last thing you need now is alcohol. Caffeine, too. They'll both mess up your body clock."

"What is this ginger stuff, then? It's not really beer?"

"No. It's like ginger ale, only better. You'll see."

As they ate, Tracy roused somewhat, and she became more aware of her surroundings. "How old is this place? It looks ancient."

Christopher leaned against the high-backed bench. "They say Cromwell slept here in the 1600's, you know, during their Civil War. But the original inn later burned down and they rebuilt it in the old style about a hundred years ago."

"I see..."

He cleared his throat. "I have a question for you, Tracy Anne."

The use of both names made her sit up straight. "And I have a few for you myself." In spite of her saucy tone, she wasn't sure she could ask the most burning one.

He sent her a lazy smile. "Ladies first."

"Chris, don't give me that old-fashioned stuff. It's a liberated world. You asked first, so shoot."

"Okay, lady. What happened to Fresh Focus? When I called, you said it was suddenly a mess, and with your talents and dedication, and, uh, reputation, I can't imagine what went sour."

Part I: Tracy

"It's a long, bad story, but it happened fast. Basically, my judgment of character went to pot and I got ripped off, then shut down by the IRS."

He shook his head. "Hey, slow down. How on earth?"

She avoided his eyes. "Well, I hired Drake Flint..."

"What?"

"Yeah, I did." She looked down at her hands. "I—I guess I let feelings cloud my decision, because a couple of people had warned me about taking him on."

"But he's a clever salesman?"

"Too clever. He had an impressive portfolio and client list, and sold me on skills he didn't have. Then botched jobs for several of my best accounts."

Christopher nodded. "I can imagine. He and I worked on a project several years ago, and he screwed up badly and threw all the heat in my direction. I ended up his scapegoat and got taken off the project."

"But that's not all." Tracy picked at a hangnail. "I found out he was—messing around with my payroll clerk. Together they diverted thousands of dollars in payroll taxes to their own use, and the IRS got none. With penalties and interest, it put Fresh Focus completely under. I learned about all this on a Thursday afternoon, and when I went to the office Friday morning, they'd already padlocked it. I couldn't even get my antique desk moved out." A dry ache caught at her throat and she couldn't say anymore.

He reached across the old oak table and took her hand. "I don't know how to put this, but my brother told me Drake had been staying in your apartment some." His voice was soft, too soft, as he tread dangerous territory. "I didn't know about all the rest."

Her eyebrows came together in a tight line. "So, Chris Mayfield, just go ahead and call me stupid, and trashy, too, while you're at it." She jerked herself up suddenly and went to stand by the fire, stiff and defiant. Then she bent her face and covered it with her hands. Firelight played on her hair.

Christopher eased up beside her, hiding his hand in the shiny locks.

His touch zinged her senses. She murmured, "And a fool, because the only one I ever loved was you—and I threw you away."

Ever so gently, he said, "I'm here now. You're here. It is possible to forgive, and to start over. If you're willing." He drew a ragged breath and spoke against her hair. "I sure am. Nothing has hurt so much as last Christmas Eve, when you refused my engagement ring, said you wanted to be your own person. I know you don't want to go through the agony of a marriage like your parents, turning children into pawns of power, but our love's not like that! We have a lot to build on."

She turned. Tears welled up before her body began shaking. "I'm scared."

"Anne, you're safe with me." His arms closed around her.

"You—you don't understand. My panic attacks are worse. They come harder and more often. I thought I was going to pass out on the flight, then again on the train from London. My world is shrinking." Her body tensed in his embrace. "If it keeps up, I could wind up afraid to come out of my bedroom. I've read about people like that, Christopher!"

He drew her tighter and rubbed her back. "I'm so sorry. Maybe we can find someone here who knows specifically how to treat that."

"I've tried several doctors and I'm getting nowhere. It was terrifying to travel here—but staying back at home was worse!"

Christopher's eyebrows went up.

She spilled the rest. "Drake is stalking me, making threatening phone calls. I find cigarette butts in the bushes

Part I: Tracy

outside my bedroom window. He followed me to a friend's house and called there. He tells me exactly what I've been doing, where I've been. He says he'll follow me—anywhere—if I report him to the authorities." Her voice dropped. "And I've already reported him."

A muscle worked in Christopher's jaw. "Then if he gets to you, it'll have to be through me first."

Tracy hiccoughed. "That's just it. I don't want you hurt again—by me or anybody else. I—I should never have come." She pushed with both hands against his chest. "Take me home, now, wherever that is."

A log on the fire shifted and sent a brilliant shower of sparks up the chimney.

The couple left the inn. Christopher led Tracy just a short walk down the lane to the old village manse, now a bed and breakfast operated by trusted friends.

Before she collapsed in dead exhaustion, Tracy wondered, *Why didn't he take me to his own cottage for the night?*

Chapter Three

Tracy woke the next morning to the smell of burnt toast. She walked down the hall to take a tub bath. A few minutes later, she pulled the stopper and reached for the towel warming on the radiator.

The voice of her hostess came through the door. "Good morning, love. Your Mr. Montgomery rang and said he'd be by for breakfast in ten minutes."

"Thank you."

She met Christopher downstairs in the dining room. He pulled out a Windsor chair and seated her at the refectory table. Conversation was sparse, as they ate the bacon and fried eggs. Questions tumbled through Tracy's mind as she spread orange marmalade on the toast, but she deliberately set them aside.

Other guests of the manse sat too nearby.

When Christopher proposed a quick tour of his office, her professional curiosity kicked in. And it gave her an excuse not to rock the relationship boat, yet. She could just savor the tenuous new beginning.

They walked several blocks and entered a modern building. Christopher took a bundle of keys from his jeans pocket. He gave the lock a quick turn, opened the door, and stood back.

He motioned Tracy to go in first. "Here's the TV Department. Actually, they call it Educational Technology on this side of the Atlantic."

Her eyes flicked over the racks and racks of high-tech equipment. "There's plenty here to do the job. Does that edit deck play just PAL, or is it multi-standard?"

"Sure. It'll play NTSC, too. Did you bring something with you?"

"Ever see a media person without a demo? Not that I have a company to do any new work."

"Old habits never die."

"Yeah. You can see it later, if you care. But I also brought a copy of your Easter Seals story somebody dropped at the office. I took it home weeks ago, not even realizing it was your work until the credits rolled."

"What'd you think?" Christopher leaned against the edit room wall.

"Very touching. How'd you learn to identify with those kids so well? They're powerful feature stories."

"Well, I worked during college at a state school for retarded children. What I saw day after day nearly broke my heart, but at the same time, those kids were a lot happier than most people. They trusted anyone, and gave affection so freely. And how they loved to sing! Of course, I could only play the tape recorder, but they didn't care."

"You never told me about that before."

"I didn't? Well, it was more than ten years ago."

"Wasn't it hard, to see them like that?"

"Some, yes. But the worst of all was doing the funerals."

Her heavily lashed eyes widened in surprise. "Funerals?"

"Yeah. A lot of the kids had severe disabilities that didn't let them live a long time. Here I was, just a teenage kid, hired to help in the chaplain's office, but I ended up

Part I: Tracy

doing several funerals by myself. A time or two, the parents didn't even show up." He bit his lip. "I could never understand that."

He shook his head slightly, and she looked away. Tracy's nails dug into her palms as she remembered too well the hurt of rejection in her own family.

She turned back to him. "You mean, nobody came?" Her voice was unsteady.

"Not a soul." There was pain in his blue eyes.

After an awkward silence, Tracy spoke a little too brightly. "So, where's your office?"

"Just around the corner. Here, this way."

He reached for a switch in the dark hallway and fluorescents popped to life. Leading her around a partition, he pointed to a cubbyhole. "I tried to clean it up for you," he chuckled, gesturing helplessly.

Papers angled every direction, and half-opened mail lay strewn across the small desk. On the left, stacks of videotapes teetered on a beat-up credenza. Almost hidden by the clutter was a small framed photo. She recognized it immediately.

He cleared his throat. "My home away from home."

She smiled. "Christopher, you always did need a keeper. Don't you have an assistant here?"

He shook his blond head and laughter bubbled up. "Naw. Want the job?"

Her lips tightened into a thin line.

He looked sharply at her. "Hey, Anne..."

Her eyes dropped to study the leather pumps on her feet. "That's just not very funny after what happened at Fresh Focus."

"I'm sorry. You are in a pickle, all right."

She nodded, absentmindedly twisting a curl around her index finger.

"I still don't understand why you let Drake get under your skin."

And into my bed, she thought. "It's...sort of involved."

A slight edge crept into his voice. "If you don't want to discuss it, I understand."

She felt her face growing warm and looked again toward the floor. "I—I guess I was pretty vulnerable after you left."

He reached out to lift her chin with his left hand, then touched her cheek. "I'm sorry I teased you about your briefcase yesterday." His voice was soft.

Her eyebrows arched. "My briefcase?"

"You don't remember?"

"No, but..."

"I forgot. Yesterday was sort of a time warp. Things were probably all muddled for you."

She struggled to think clearly after his touch. "As a matter of fact, I am confused about something."

He gestured to an armchair beside the stack of tapes. "Have a seat. Nobody's likely to interrupt us here."

She lowered herself into the chair, while he pulled a file folder out of the other one, plopped it on a pile, then sat down straightening his jeans.

Tracy just watched him for a moment. She thought back to the feel of his arms around her, his hands so expert in love when they were together.

He placed his hands on his knees and leaned forward. "So, what were you wondering?" His words came gently, coaxing.

She licked her wine-colored lips and leaned toward him. Then she sat back again. Her chest rose and fell beneath the smart jumper she wore. "I can't figure out where I stand with you right now."

A lost look came into her eyes, before she glanced down at her lap. She chipped a bit of nail polish off her pinkie finger with a thumbnail. "You tried to explain something last night, about secondary, ah, virginity..." She swallowed. "That's when I cratered. Why did you put me up at the bed

Part I: Tracy

and breakfast instead of taking me to your place?"

Christopher rolled his chair closer and clasped both her hands. "Anne, you can't imagine how happy I am you came." His voice grew unexpectedly husky. "You believe me, don't you?"

"Yes. You seem glad to see me. But..." She frowned slightly. "I don't know if we're picking up where we left off, or what." She pulled her hands loose and turned her palms up. Her eyes held an earnest question.

"See if this makes sense. I've been thinking a lot since our months together, since I've been here." He paused and their eyes locked. "Do you remember..." His words faltered as he leaned closer to her and caressed her smooth cheeks and luxurious, loose curls. At the familiar touch, he gently urged her head closer and covered her lips with his. One masculine hand continued to revel in the feel of her abundant hair.

Tracy held back, tense at first, but his lips claimed hers with increasing pressure, until the pulse spot in her neck pounded.

Slowly, Christopher stood and drew Tracy out of the chair. His arms pressed against her back to urge their bodies together.

She ached with remembered pleasure and sighed softly as she hugged him in return. Their thighs touched lightly at the same time she again gave him the sweetness of her mouth. Unbidden images of their earlier lovemaking descended with furious speed on her mind in a kaleidoscope of desire. Yes, she remembered, all right, how good they'd been together.

All at once, Christopher released her and sat down roughly. His head rested on his hands. "I can't..."

Tracy teetered a moment, then regained her balance. Flushed from passion, she glared at the bent, blond head.

"You—can't—what?" Hands on hips, she nearly spat

the words.

He didn't meet her eyes.

"What's going on, Christopher?" she demanded again, an even harder edge creeping into her voice. The toes of her high heels tapped on the linoleum floor.

Finally, he looked up, anguish in his eyes.

"I said, what's going on? I come thousands of miles at your mere phone call," she choked. "I don't even know why. My company is a mess, and I probably shouldn't have left. Nobody's giving me vacation pay! But I use precious savings to get to this little burg. You feed me, drop me off at some friends, and all I get is a goodnight peck. What kind of a game are you playing?"

"I just want our love to have the right foundation. That's why I don't think we should sleep together anymore unless we're married. It's what people call secondary virginity."

Tracy glared at him. "Good grief, Chris, what Sunday school did you just drop in from? I thought all you Texas cowboys know it's too late to close the gate once you let the cow out!" She gulped air. "And I guess you think you fooled me just now with your passionate performance!" She wheeled abruptly, then stomped out. Her heels echoed angrily through the building. *Secondary virginity! What a joke! Even if I wanted it back, that's impossible.*

When Tracy's face met the outside air, the scalding tears burst out at last. She lunged across the campus lawn toward a tree-lined lake.

* * *

Christopher turned 180 degrees in his chair, shoved a stack of papers forward, and laid his head on the desk. *That was no performance—and I can't even trust myself to do what I know is right.*

Chapter Four

Tracy found a footpath toward the lake. Her heart pounded as she ran on and on. Her lungs sucked air, and the wind began to dry her eyes. "That man!"

As she passed a huge rhododendron bush, she squeezed her eyes shut for just an instant—and tripped on a long, narrow strip of leather. The next moment, Tracy sprawled on the walkway, hard. One of her pumps flew across the grass, and someone's smashed eyeglasses landed on the gravel beside her.

Gingerly, she raised up on one elbow to inspect the shredded knees of her hose and turned to see who had witnessed her embarrassment.

At one end of the leash stood a sheepdog. His black and white fur covered a well-fed shape, and a pink tongue lolled in a friendly fashion from his grizzled mouth as he moved toward Tracy.

"Easy, boy!" At the word of his master, the dog moved back and sat on his haunches.

The owner of the proper Oxford voice—and the dog—bent down to give Tracy a hand. "Are you quite all right, Miss?"

Circle of Love

For a few seconds she couldn't speak. All she could do was stare at the stranger and his canine friend.

The aging man looked every inch a scholar. His hair was more gray than brown, and his jacket and baggy trousers sagged on an ample frame. But his necktie flapped with bold hieroglyphics, and under his craggy eyebrows was a face surprisingly tanned.

She extended her left hand to his, then drew it back. Tracy winced as she caught her breath. "I—I guess—your glasses—kept going." She tried to reach them on the ground beside her.

"Allow me." The professor bent to pick them up and dangled the frames from his free hand. One lens was cracked to pieces. He folded the glasses and casually slipped them into his trousers pocket.

"I'm so sorry. I wasn't watching." She shoved herself upward and made it to her feet. "Please, let me have them repaired for you."

He smiled. "First things first. The name is Arthur Leatherwood. I teach here. Now, how are those knees?"

She touched one gently and brushed off some tiny pebbles. "Ooh."

"Come, sit down a moment." He took her arm and led her over to an oak bench.

The dog picked up her shoe and followed them.

She reached out a hand to pat his head. "Thank you, er..."

"His name is Ramses, the best companion a fellow could...Why, you're trembling."

"I'll—I'll be okay, really I will."

But she didn't look all right. Her mascara was smeared, her voice shook, and she perched on the bench like a sparrow about to take flight.

"There, there, Miss...?"

"Stevens. Call me Tracy...or Anne"

Part I: Tracy

"You're not a student here."

"No, I've come to visit a—friend." She looked at his broken glasses. "I'm at fault for running into you. Where can I get these fixed?"

"Our first item of business is to get you patched up. Besides, I keep spare spectacles around because I'm forever misplacing them." He patted a pocket in his jacket and withdrew some half-glasses. "See?"

Tracy leaned against the bench and stuck her legs straight out in front of her. With her long nails she reached out to pull the hosiery away from her scraped knees. Her hand still trembled violently.

"Miss Stevens..."

"I—I'm all right, really. I've lived through skinned knees before. Though it was an awfully long time ago." She gave a wry smile. "It's just..." She swallowed. "I'm—I'm having some confusing things going on in my life right now."

Ramses edged closer and laid his head against the side of her leg.

As Tracy talked with Leatherwood and curled her fingers through Ramses' fur, she began to relax a little.

"Not to pry, but is there anything I can do to help? I do like to converse with the young people on campus here. So many of them are looking for meaning and direction." He gazed out at the lake and ran his hand through his thinning hair.

Tracy waited, listening to the gentle breeze in the trees and resting her eyes on the calm lake.

When he spoke again, it was more to himself than to her. "Ah, youth. All that energy, but sometimes the frenzy just hides the searching. I'm not at all convinced I'd want to experience it over again." He put his hand on Ramses' graying muzzle. "Yet before long I'll be put on the shelf like a moldy piece of something ancient. My colleagues seem to make all the brilliant discoveries and write the important books, while I'll probably get put out to pasture before my time. Just once before I retire, I'd like to unearth something truly valuable..."

The professor's eyebrows drew together. "Hrummph. Here I am waxing philosophical, while you're in need of cleaning up and a bandage, young lady!" Leatherwood stood, one hand with the leash and his other extended to Tracy. "Come, let's have the Health Centre take a look at you."

"If you don't mind, I'd rather go to Educational Technology. That's where my, uh, friend is."

"Very well."

They strolled slowly along the walk, with Ramses waddling alongside.

"And whom might you know in Ed Tech, Miss Stevens?"

"Christopher Montgomery." Just saying his name made her uncomfortable. "You probably don't know him. He's just here for a semester."

The professor quirked a brow. "As a matter of fact, I have met him. That young Texan has already added a bit of a tang to my life. A fine young fellow." He chuckled to himself. "Though he's still getting used to milk in his tea!"

"I'm here on a short visit, and we just had a, uh, difference of opinion." Tracy's soft voice almost cracked. "That's why I—ran into you."

"I see." His brown eyes filled with sympathy. He and Tracy were silent the remainder of the walk to the building.

Christopher was just coming down the steps when he saw them. His somber face brightened. "Professor Leatherwood!" His wave stopped in the middle. "Anne! I was coming to look for you."

The professor cleared his throat. "I believe this young lady needs a bit of attention."

Chris frowned as he met Tracy Anne's gaze. With a

Part I: Tracy

sheepish grin, she pointed to her knees.

"Good grief! Did old Ramses here wrap his leash around you?"

"No, I ran smack-dab into him—and the professor, too."

A smile almost leaked from the corner of Chris' mouth, but he covered it quickly with his hand. "Thank you, sir, for bringing her back here. I'll take her to my place for a little first aid."

"I can take care of it, Christopher." Tracy straightened her shoulders. "Really, it doesn't amount to much." She started to turn toward the village.

"It's the least I can do, Anne." He took her left hand firmly and squeezed it.

"Okay, Chris."

Christopher turned. "Thanks, sir."

Tracy shook Leatherwood's hand. "You've been so kind. I hope to see you around campus again." She paused. "And—I hope you find—exactly what you're looking for."

A knowing smile crossed the gentleman's face. He bent down to scratch Ramses between the ears, then straightened slowly and gave her a nod. "Miss Stevens, I hope you do, too."

* * *

In the deep of night, Tracy rolled over in bed. She seemed to hear the distant double ring of an English phone.

Her hostess tapped on her door and motioned for Tracy to come to the telephone booth in the hall.

The voice over the satellite delay was unmistakable. "I know where you are, Tracy. If you don't hurt me, I won't have to hurt you." There came a click, then nothing.

For a long time afterward, Tracy lay under the comforter, shaking. Her eyes raked every corner of the chintz bedroom, and finally she fell into a troubled sleep.

The next morning, Tracy sat alone at the table and let her breakfast get cold.

The manse lady bustled over with a fresh pot of tea. "Aren't you hungry this fine morning, dear?"

"Did—did you call me to the phone late last night?" Tracy added sugar to her tea and stirred mindlessly.

She looked curiously at her guest. "No. In fact, I slept especially well. Nobody was needing anything."

Tracy put down the teaspoon and sagged in her chair. Relief washed over her face. "Thank God."

But the words of the dream continued to haunt her.

* * *

After lunch, Christopher held the pub door, as Tracy emerged into the daylight. "It's too early to set up for the next class yet. Are your knees up to a walk around the village?"

"I think so." She blinked, even in the soft afternoon light. "And, by the way, thanks for helping me through that ploughman's lunch. I could never have eaten that slab of cheese by myself."

"Sure." He turned into a narrow lane and gestured for her to follow. "Here's the path I take when I need time out of the center just to think."

"I never had a lunch getaway like this at the ad agency." She tossed her hair, but her laugh was a little brittle.

"I know. I've about decided that's part of the problem. Chasing the bucks in a feeding frenzy just isn't as important to me as it used to be."

"That's fine for you. This is a pretty cushy little assignment for you for the time being. Then what?"

He looked serious. "That's still what I'm trying to figure out." He pointed to a row of houses behind neat little fences. "In spite of the crooked roads around here, these places just

Part I: Tracy

stand here without much change, all laid out as they have been for several hundred years."

"Uh, huh. And I think it's kind of charming."

"Well, sure. The village is. But my personal goals are higgledy-piggledy in comparison. I don't mind a few twists and turns, but I'd like to know generally where I'm going."

She stopped to face him. "So, don't you?"

"No." He turned his head away. "Not anymore. In fact, there's a lot I'm not sure of anymore."

She took hold of his arm. "Such as..."

"Climbing the corporate ladder, doing most everything for myself." He took a breath and turned toward her face. "And you."

Her eyebrows arched. "Me? You're having an early mid-life crisis partly because of me?"

The life was missing from his laugh. "Well, not entirely you. Besides our split up, there's all that get-all-you-can, look-out-for-number-one stuff in our industry back in the States—well, I'm really disillusioned, that's all."

"Count me in, too. I just got the rip-off of my life."

"That's a classic understatement. Drake's a jerk, and I hope he really has to pay big-time for what he did."

"Meanwhile, I've got to pay the IRS. Got any good ideas on finding a decent job when I go back?"

He brushed the comment aside. "I'd rather not talk about your going back."

"I will, you know. It's inevitable."

He slowed his pace somewhat. "Well, I hope it's not. Maybe you'll find something here—or someone—that makes you decide to stay."

"But for how long? You admit yourself you don't know what's next." There was chiding in her tone. "What made you so unsure all of a sudden, Chris? You always seemed to have the world by the tail."

"I haven't told you about it yet. But there was this documentary we shot in the mountains of Central America. I saw life like I'd never seen it before. And I saw death, too, right before my eyes."

She gave him a sympathetic look. "Well, it does happen. We see it nightly on the news."

"But I've never been in the room. The life just—went away." His voice cracked.

She took his hand gently. "Tell me about it."

They found a bench on the village green and sat down there.

"Well, not long after I moved out, I got a call to work on this production in Guatemala. We flew up into the Highlands in a little Cessna and landed on a dirt strip not far from the Mexican border."

She leaned back slightly. "Not very typical of the projects you take on."

"You can say that again. We walked with our camera gear into this town and passed women beating their wash on the river rocks. The people were Maya Indians, fairly shy but very colorful. I felt like I'd been dumped onto the pages of *National Geographic!*"

"So, what else happened?"

"After we shot the interviews and B-roll footage we came for, someone came running in to say an emergency case was coming into the clinic. A caesarean delivery, and did we want to get a few shots of that."

"And you couldn't resist getting that just-one-more shot?"

He grinned sheepishly. "You know me well. That's right. The camera crew went a few blocks away to this clinic that only the year before had gotten screens on the windows."

"You're kidding."

"I'm not. But it was remarkably well-equipped and staffed, for the simple facility it was. Anyway, they brought

Part I: Tracy

in this Indian lady who had been in labor since the day before at a government clinic that couldn't do surgery. This mission clinic was their last hope. But she bounced in a car on dirt roads for four more hours to get there."

"Then what?"

"The Ladino doctor and a couple of nurses prepared everything quickly. I was elected to run camera in the operating room. When I saw the patient, I was shocked. She was no bigger than our twelve-year-old neighbor back home. Even her feet sticking out from under the sheets were tiny. She seemed like a child herself battling for this baby, even though they told me she was at least twenty."

"So, what happened?"

"The medical team stood in a circle and prayed first, then gave her a general anesthetic—something used a lot in Latin America that's not even legal in the U.S.—and quickly but carefully opened her up. When they penetrated the uterus, blood and fluid gushed up in the air and all over the floor. And it wasn't long before the doctor lifted out the baby. He was really purple, but when they used a bulb syringe to suction him out, he let out a feeble wail."

"Then?"

"That was all. The nurse wrapped him warmly and carried him into the next room to the counter to work with him. But there were no more cries. Only silence. They did everything they could to stimulate him to keep breathing. But he never made another sound."

"And the mother was still under?"

"Yeah. She never even got to hear her son's only cry." He shook his head. "I still can't figure out why it got to me so bad. I mean, It wasn't fair. It wasn't his fault. Maybe if he'd been born somewhere with a neonatal unit and all sorts of technology available, he'd have had a chance!"

"Did they ever say what they thought the trouble was?"

"Only that they thought the father had syphilis—but the

baby hadn't done anything wrong. And they had prayed. I mean, they asked God to help them and He let them down."

"Maybe that's what's eating you more than anything."

"What?"

"The part about God. You thought He'd come through. Yet He let you down and let the baby die right in front of you."

"Maybe it is. He's let me down lately, it seems. Several things."

"Maybe you've let this God of yours down. And not the other way around. I know your parents didn't approve of our lifestyle when we lived together, and if you go for all that God stuff then maybe that's why you're feeling some of this. Not just seeing the baby not make it."

"Well, you certainly didn't mind having me move in!" There was a harder tone in his response.

"Hey, don't blame it on me! You really pushed, and, yeah, well, I was really attracted to you and wanted to try it out."

"Was attracted?"

She stood up and walked off down the lane. He followed her.

"Oh, come on Christopher! I still am—why else would I get on that red-eye special and come here to tramp around the woods and moldy old houses with you! I could be back home networking myself into a way to pay my debts. In fact, I think I should go home and do just that!"

He put a hand on her shoulder and turned her to face him.

"Anne." She saw her own hurt mirrored in his eyes. "Why is it that whenever we talk about something really important, it ends up in some kind of a fight?"

"I—I don't know." The insides of her eyelids felt funny, so she turned away and kept walking. "I just don't know."

He fell in step beside her and they wound their way

Part I: Tracy

through the village streets in complete silence. Her shoulders drooped.

Without warning, loud tones split the air. She jerked her head up toward the treetops. "What's that?"

"Oh, it's just the bells."

The sound struck again, a strong beat, then the fast rush of other notes falling downward. Then another and another.

"Just the bells?" Her eyes came alive. "I've never heard anything like it in my life!"

He spoke louder to carry over the competition. "Well, folks around here have been hearing them all their lives. They're just part of the natural rhythm of things."

She stood motionless and listened. Peal after peal of the music cascaded through the treetops onto the street where she stood. "Well, I like it," she murmured. Then she brightened again. "Where are they coming from? Can we go see?" The questions rushed out at once.

Christopher laughed as he pointed. "Over there. And yes, let's go." He grabbed her hand and took off running.

Just around the next turn in the lane, they came to an old stone church. While the air resounded with a musical litany, they paused on the sidewalk and looked upward toward the belfry. As Tracy's face turned skyward, her whole being seemed to open up to the pealing bells. And soak up the sound as a thirsty sponge.

"That's the most beautiful sound I've ever heard in my life." Something faint in her memory began to stir. As she listened, she consciously tried to coax it out. Full minutes went by as she continued to feel the music, as if it were cleansing her soul.

Then the image snapped into focus. A weekend at her grandparents' country church, when she got to pull the single bell rope all by herself. Those few days away from the battleground of her own parents, when she felt the warmth of real love. A gentle touch, a sweet song to sleep by, a lap full of hugs, and days of funny stories and laughter. What's she's wanted to find again all her life.

She grabbed Chris' jacket, totally unaware of the tears on her cheeks. "Look, I've got to go inside and watch. Do you know the way to the belfry?"

Startled, he stammered, "Uh, okay. Sure—but I can't take you to the belfry itself."

"Why not?"

"It's dangerous up there. Your ears can't stand it. But I can show you where the bell room is. The ringers are definitely practicing this afternoon!"

She called back to him, "That's good enough. Let's go." By the time he caught up, she was at the door, fumbling with the ancient hardware.

"Here. Let me try. I've had a little more practice with these things."

"Hurry!" There was a curious urgency in her voice.

Tracy scarcely sensed the passage of time as she and Christopher looked in on the ringers and watched them work. A slice of joy, recaptured from childhood, reached deep into her heart.

Chapter Five

Late that afternoon, Tracy visited one of Christopher's classes. Then, after dinner at the refectory, he showed her the faculty lounge.

She looked around at the comfortable room. "Nice place, but where is everybody?"

"All gone home or grading papers in their offices, I'd expect. Say, would you like to sit down, or are you too tired to hang around awhile?"

"I'm fine." She sat on one end of a leather couch. "I enjoyed sitting in on the class this afternoon. You do a good job, Chris. And it's obvious you enjoy what you're teaching."

"Well, thanks. I can get excited about it, when I don't think about the down side or what I need to do next."

"You don't really seem to need a team teacher. Me or anybody else."

"Sure I do. And you saw the mess in my office." His reply was a little too quick.

"Christopher, you're trying to manipulate me into staying."

"Who, me?" He broke into a grin as he lunged toward her. "Manipulate? Never. But I'll tickle you to death until you promise to do it!"

She laughed and squirmed as his hands found her vulnerable spots, those places his hands knew well from the love games they used to play.

"Help! Stop! I'm staying." She stopped laughing and pushed against his chest. "Chris, I said I am staying!"

He stopped abruptly and removed his hands from her delectable ribs. His eyes widened. "You are?"

"I am."

"When did you decide that?" He rushed on. "And why didn't you tell me?"

"Well, because the time wasn't right yet." Her lips pouted impishly.

"And now it is?"

"Guess so. Besides, the tickle bug made me tell you."

He gave her a quick squeeze. "God bless the tickle bug."

Before she gave herself time to back down, she blurted, "Whether you need me to help in class or not, I've decided to learn change ringing. Every well-rounded person needs to know how to ring church bells." A grin teased the corners of her lips.

Christopher sat up straight and scrutinized her face. "Did I miss something?" His head tipped to the side in puzzlement. "Anne, what happened this afternoon?"

"What do you mean?"

"The thing about the bells. Something happened to you because of them. What was it?"

She looked down at her painted nails and picked at a cuticle. "Well, it's—it's hard to explain. I'm not even too sure myself yet. I think it has something to do with going to my grandparents' farm. I visited often on weekends when I was really little. Later, I lived with them all the time after the divorce. That's when I was about eight."

"And?"

"I, I think maybe it was the only place I ever felt loved,

Part I: Tracy

just for myself. Not because of anything I did, or achieved. You already know my life with my parents was a real mess, but today I remembered a time when I felt secure and accepted. And it was those times at Grampy and Gramma's, when they let me ring the church bell." She kept her eyes focused on her hands.

"So—hearing the bells today brought it back?"

"I guess so. You see, they died by the time I was eleven. But I know they really loved me. I may have been young, but I knew. Even though I can't even remember a time consciously thinking about that since I grew up. Maybe that's why..." She looked at him, then interrupted herself with a shake of the head.

"Why what?"

Her face closed. "Never mind. It's not anything important."

"Somehow I think it is. You've ducked into your shell away from me, Anne." He leaned over to stroke the hand she was studying so closely.

She hesitated a long time, then rushed out her answer all in a breath. "Well, maybe that's why when I get depressed I like to imagine this big happy tree, all safe underneath, that I can hide under and feel secure." She took a deep breath and straightened her skirt. "Now, that sounds stupid coming from a grown woman, doesn't it?"

There was compassion in his eyes. "No, Anne, it doesn't sound that way at all. It sounds like a hurt little girl who's grown up to take on the world but needs a safe spot to be herself." He touched her face and leaned close. His lips brushed hers as he put his arms around her. Into her hair, he spoke. "Could I share your tree? It sounds nice. I'd like to sit under it with you."

Her shoulders began to shake. Tears spilled down her face. "But I don't know where it is!"

He continued to hold her as she sobbed. "We'll find it,

my precious Anne. Somehow, some way, we'll find it together."

Chapter Six

Anne crept into the back of the stone church. "Brrr, it's chilly in here." She drew her sweater tighter.

A sacristy door opened and the vicar waved to her. "This way, Anne, to the practice. You're just in time!" His blue eyes crinkled at the corners, and he looked younger in the face than his silvered hair suggested. "I'm glad you've come. The verger told me you wanted to learn the bells."

She nodded. "At least, I hope to try."

They climbed the narrow stone steps to the ringing room, where a circle of people stood, giant ropes in hand. Velvet sleeves wrapped a section of each rope. The vicar formally introduced Tracy Anne to the group.

A sturdy woman stepped forward. "My name's Sarah. Here's the way you grasp it, then pull." She placed Tracy's hands in proper position. "We'll teach you simple patterns first, and after awhile you'll catch on to the technique."

"I had no idea it was so complicated," Anne responded.

"Actually, it is quite mathematical, when you look at the art closely. Well determined patterns, each with a name, and so on," Sarah explained.

Tracy turned toward the vicar. "And even the bells them-

Circle of Love

selves have names?"

"Yes, many do." He tugged a rope attached to the massive oak frame, and the giant wheel overhead turned. The belfry resonated. "That's Paul the Apostle. He was cast in 1599 by Joseph Carter's foundry in Reading and carries the inscription 'Prayes the Lord.' The key is E major. Here, let's ring him again."

He placed Anne's hand firmly on the rope's velvet sleeve, and led her through the rhythmical tug. The wheel overhead rotated the great tenor bell, and "Paul" echoed pure and strong.

A smile of satisfaction lit her face, then she wrinkled her brow. "He's beautiful. But how on earth do you know the right timing for each ring, to get the blended sound of each pattern?"

Sarah smiled. "Ah, it takes timing and practice to learn the peal of six we use. 'Tisn't learned in a day."

"You have such patience, to keep up an art form like this, when a lot of folks back home just don't bother anymore with history and tradition. Why do you do it?"

Sarah looked upward, then straight at Tracy. "It is admirable to keep up such a fine tradition, handed down over hundreds of years. But there's much more to it than that. To a man, I'd say our ringers do it, not out of duty or tradition, but to the glory of God."

She mused, "The glory of God."

"Indeed," added the vicar. "Beauty to reflect his comeliness, and faithfulness in calling men—ah, and women—to attend worship and experience his presence and work in their lives. Is that not the purpose of every human being?"

"I'd never thought that way about it before."

When the practice ended, Anne left the portals of the stone church, still pondering the ringer's words. *Living for someone else's glory? That's a foreign idea in more ways than one.*

Chapter Seven

Christopher took Anne's hand in his, as they walked down the campus path to the old manor house. "Since the humanities classes have ended for the day, it's a perfect time for the tour of Keele Hall I've been promising you."

Together, they entered the gates and crossed the cobblestone courtyard. Tracy Anne's eyes widened. Up close, the seventeenth-century home seemed larger than life. Its scale and grandeur eclipsed any family dwelling she'd ever imagined. A heraldic shield, with a *fleur-de-lis* and scythe design, decorated an alcove between two tall windows. Up high, Latin inscriptions encircled the walls in the shadow of the eaves. Stone lions guarded each pinnacle of the multi-angled roof, which sprouted more chimneypots than Tracy Anne could easily count.

Christopher pointed toward the formal front entrance. "About forty years ago, the government took over care of the house, renaming it and starting the university. The manor was built in 1580, during the reign of Queen Elizabeth I. That's her coat of arms just below the oriel window."

The couple stood still, poised on the threshold of the

servants' entrance. The wings of the immense sandstone house literally wrapped around them.

He turned the hammered iron hardware on the oak door. Beneath the motto, "Thanke God for All" carved in the lintel, they stepped into the past.

Christopher turned right, toward the vast rooms on the first floor. Tracy followed. Their quiet footfalls made the only sound in the hallway. Everywhere lingered the scent of aged wood, a whisper of long ago.

Tall double doors squeaked on their hinges, as Chris led her through them. He put his arm around her waist and gave her a sideways hug. She smiled warmly in surprise. They spoke little, but when they did, their words were hushed, almost reverent, as they began to explore the main floor rooms.

He held her hand tightly through the oak-paneled hallway. To the left appeared a vision of white and gold leaf, decorated in columns and faded floral tapestry. "This is the breakfast room," he said as they entered it.

They passed through that airy room into a shadowed, deep-toned space. Crimson drapes let in slices of light that struck handcrafted paneling and carvings of fruit and flowers. "Behold, the dining room," Christopher announced.

"Can you imagine eating here by candlelight?" Tracy's voice was soft.

"Mmmm. I think it would be nice, with just a modest table for two, that is." Chris bowed in knightly fashion and kissed her hand with a flourish.

Her eyes sparkled when she returned the gesture with a mock curtsey. She walked over to the fireplace and looked up at the cracking portrait there. An austere man stared down, his neck encased in an Elizabethan ruff. "I wonder about the people who lived in this house, how they loved and hated, hoped and feared. Deep down, were they anything like us—or worlds apart?"

Part I: Tracy

"Hmmm. From Shakespeare to the space shuttle. In nearly four hundred years a lot of things change, but I tend to think human nature stays the same."

Tracy's hand traced a bouquet of roses carved below the mantel. "So you think they had the same struggles as we do, just in a different context?"

"Yeah, I do."

"Well, I'll have to mull that over. Life seems so complicated today."

"Each era had its own challenges, I'd imagine." He cleared his throat. "Now, how about seeing more of the house?"

"Sure. It certainly has an aura all its own."

Passing back through the breakfast room, they rounded a corner. "Here's the family library." Christopher ushered Tracy into a spacious room filled with ancient volumes gathered over centuries. "Professor Leatherwood told me the earliest books—the few that survived the Roundheads' pillaging during the Civil War—were moved years ago to the university archives. But it's still quite a collection."

From the marble fireplace Chris and Tracy turned toward a breathtaking view of the lawn and gardens.

Christopher moved to a corner of the room. He gestured for her to go on up the spiral stair. Right behind her, he climbed through the narrow passage, to emerge on the second level gallery.

When he showed her the door camouflaged with cut-off book backs, she laughed and hurried down to view it from the main level. "How clever!"

At last, their tour led them to the grand staircase. Chris stopped and placed his hand on a carved newel post.

Tracy pressed her back against the opposite wall. "These steps must be ten or twelve feet across!"

He tilted his head upward. "And look how the windows in the tower light it. What a dramatic location!"

"Film and video forever on the brain, huh, Chris?" But she found herself wondering how it would feel to descend these stairs dressed in velvet and lace, like an English version of Scarlett O'Hara. Or perhaps a kinder lady.

His eyes rested on one of the portraits on the wall. A serene gentleman with long hair and a close-cropped beard held a plumed hat in his lap; his Cavalier clothing shone like silk. "Imagine living here then."

Late afternoon light slanted in, and as if by magic the dust particles danced.

"Oh, Chris. You were right. It is a special place." Tracy reached over and gave him a quick kiss, and pulled him up the steps. "C'mon. Show me the rest."

Stair carpet softened their footsteps. They reached the top and found themselves in a wide minstrel gallery.

With his arm around her shoulders, the couple leaned over the gallery railing. They peered down at the medieval Great Hall, with its hulking fireplace and stained glass windows. And followed the gallery's giant U-shape until they found themselves opposite the staircase.

Suddenly, the walkway ceased. Before them beckoned a plain but mysterious door.

Christopher moved toward the iron latch. "I never noticed this before. Where could it lead, I wonder?"

This time, Anne hesitated. "I—I'm not sure we should go in there." Her stomach fluttered, as if—somehow—setting foot beyond that door committed her, might even change her life's direction.

But Christopher shrugged his shoulders. "Why not?" He creaked the door open and stepped inside. She followed timidly.

It was a small room unlike any other in the house. The strange space held only a battered writing desk and chair. But the windows! They formed a gentle arc across one side of the room. Shafts of golden light refracted through

Part I: Tracy

hundreds of diamond-shaped panes of glass.

"This hideaway must be..." Christopher turned around in a slow circle and faced the glass again. "This room lies behind the oriel window."

Drawn by the warmth, the intimacy here, Anne stepped closer, grasping Christopher's hand. *What secrets did this room know? What stories could it tell? What tales of love—or lost love—did it witness?* Tracy Anne felt a pressure on her chest, almost as if someone squeezed her heart.

She looked down at the cobblestone courtyard. It had been empty earlier, but now she wasn't so sure. Some kind of movement seemed to shimmer there. Though the brilliant light stung her eyelids, she stood staring for a long time.

She hardly noticed Christopher waiting quietly, just watching.

Clouds blew across the sun, casting streaks of shadow into the room. Tracy reached out and touched her fingertips to the glass. A drowning sense of separation washed over her.

She turned back toward the man.

He sucked in his breath and stood still as stone. It was her face. The slashes of gloom on her countenance. Her skin caught the strange light, and upon it lay a haunting sadness.

"Christopher. Now I know what I have to do. Tomorrow, I'll make plans to travel home."

A weight crushed his chest. "No!" He reached for her.

"It's been a good try, but the relationship isn't going to work, not the way you want it to."

"No! You haven't given us a fair chance. We need more time." He shook his head. His arms tightened.

"I have to go. I can't imprison you, too, in my struggle." She leaned back from his embrace and brushed her thumb against his beard. "But Christopher—you will always have a—a unique place in my heart." She closed her eyes a moment against the hurt she saw in his. "Because of—

knowing you—loving you, I will never be the same again."

 Something moved again in the courtyard. Tracy Anne turned from him toward the window. And she tasted tears.

Part II: Honour

Chapter Eight

Mayfield Manor, August 1642

The raven-haired beauty pressed her face to the leaded panes of the oriel window. "Godspeed, Father," she whispered, as unbidden tears spilled onto her velvet gown.

The man she lived for—still robust and dashing—turned just then in his saddle and waved his wide-brimmed hat. "Long live King Charles!" he shouted, his enthusiasm apparently undampened, though his hat plumes already grew limp in the mist.

Robert Mayfield squared his shoulders within the scarlet coat. The newest member of the King's Lifeguards adjusted his weapons, planted high boots in the stirrups, then spurred his dark bay through the stone portals of the manor. His retainers followed. As evergreens swallowed up the small party, a growing ache for the leader caught at Honour's heart.

The ripening girl of seventeen years clutched the journal to her young breasts and laid her palm against the glass. *I fear nothing shall ever be the same again.*

* * *

Circle of Love

Pale rays slanted into the Great Hall, illuminating mother and daughter as they sewed quietly beside the fire.

Honour jumped at a sudden clatter of boots on the grand staircase, and pierced herself with the needle. "Oooh." She put her fingertip to her lips. "How long shall this new outrage continue? Parliament prepares to cross swords with its own king and countrymen, while my brother defends some foreign cause!"

She jabbed the offending tool into the fabric and sat forward on the marquetry chair. "Father is gone to Nottingham. Andrew fights on the Continent, God knows where. The servants are wary. And now soldiers swarm our lands—and even the house—like bees." Honour stretched her finger in the direction of the noise. "And narry a half-penny we shall get in return, I wager, whatever His Majesty promises."

"True, true, daughter, but we have no say." Catherine adjusted her wide lace collar, then picked up her needlework again. "Your father hath been faithful to the King since childhood. He can do naught else but defend His Majesty's sovereignty." She reached into a drawstring purse suspended from the waist of her dress and withdrew a linen handkerchief. "My heart likewise is heavy without his presence." She touched the cloth to the corner of one eye. "Heavy, indeed."

Honour rose from the carved chair. Her skirts swished against the stone floor. She leaned over to place a kiss on Catherine's cheek. "Perhaps Father and my brother shall return to us by spring, this dreadful business over."

"I pray so." Catherine's hands shook as she resumed stitching.

A servant entered with a trencher of bread, fruit, and a small cut of cold venison.

The girl eyed the selection sharply. "The larder grows poorer by the day, with all these unwanted soldiers about."

Quietly came Catherine's reply. "One day you may

Part II: Honour

thank God for their protection."

Honour, dark brows drawn together, mumbled a response as she selected an apple and moved toward the carved doors.

"Where are you going?"

"To the stables. I have not laid eyes on Snowflake this day."

Catherine's eyes softened. "Wear your cloak, then."

"I shall."

The girl's steps lightened on the cobblestones as she neared the stables. She entered the dark structure and went straight for the stall that held her own mount, a well-bred horse fifteen hands high, with a dash of Eastern blood. The swish of a tail and a strong whinny greeted her. Honour caressed the white marking on the Barbary mare's head.

"You are becoming a beauty, just as Father judged. How I wish he could see you!"

A fresh pain struck her heart. She almost felt the rain-damp air of that recent morning when her father brought Snowflake to the manor. "Come! See the surprise!" With long steps outdistancing hers, he had hurried her to the stables, excitement in his eyes.

"A lady nigh to seventeen years needs her own special mount. 'Tis some early, I know, but a gentleman ought not leave in the King's service, neglecting a suitable birthday gift to his only daughter." Beneath a handsome mustache, his mouth curved into a benevolent smile.

Honour had always felt great affection for her father, but never more than at that moment. The sparkle had danced from his eyes to hers, and impulsively she had hugged him around the middle.

"Oh, Father!" She had let loose of him and started to dance a circle in the straw. Mid-step she halted.

"Leave in the King's service?" Fingers of fear threatened her voice. Her questioning eyes found his.

"Aye. Discontent festers in our country. Events unfold against our Sovereign that grow bolder by the day. Mobs in London yell 'Privilege of Parliament' and strip the Lord Mayor of his office. He already joins the Archbishop in the Tower of London. Even the Queen flees to Holland to raise money and arms." He lowered his voice. "While His Majesty has doubtless made errors in judgment, I cannot abandon him."

Honour had stood rigid with shock, as he reached for her.

"It wounds me to put distance betwixt us, and even more to trouble your young heart. God help you to understand. Aye, I must depart. This midday."

"No! No!" she had screamed. "First Andrew, then you!"

Honour's right hand wound tightly in the horse's mane, as she laid her face against the warm neck. "No," she echoed, remembering. "Not Father, too."

After awhile, Snowflake nuzzled the girl's other hand and found the apple. Honour wiped tears against her equine friend, then sniffed.

"Yea, you discovered my treat. You shall have it." The girl stroked the dark animal, relishing their mutual bond.

Chapter Nine

On the last day of August, a messenger rode into the royal encampment at Nottingham. He dismounted and whisked the message pouch off his horse. Within moments, he would stand in the presence of the King.

His Majesty, King Charles, relaxed in his favorite chair, a carved sling-back with leather seat. Fit and able in his early forties, he wore unadorned silk, a loose-fitting doublet and hose. A broad, lace-edged collar reached his shoulders. His Majesty's wide-brimmed beaver hat lay on a trunk beside him.

Nearby sat two of his noble advisors and members of the Lifeguards, Sir Robert Mayfield and Sir Edmund Verney. In a moment of levity with these friends of his youth, the King leaned back laughing, shook his long curled hair, and fingered his wispy mustache.

Soon as the messenger was announced, the royal one grew serious. He pulled out a key from the breast of his jerkin, as he grasped the communication pouch, then opened up the lock. Quickly, he scanned the documents it contained and laid them aside.

"Have you anything else to report of how the gentry

leans in Cheshire? Do they remain loyal to us or revolt with Parliament?"

The young man looked a moment at the ground. "There is something, your Most Gracious Majesty, but..."

"Go on."

"I fear it will bring you great displeasure."

King Charles leaned forward. "Out with it!"

"Two days ago the village of Barthomley was attacked. The townspeople fled to the church for safe haven, and it was put to the torch. The pews, straw flooring, and even the church tower were set aflame."

All three listeners frowned.

"Seventeen men were forced out of the building. Their enemies removed all their clothes and promised them freedom. Then slaughtered a dozen of them."

Sir Robert smacked his hand with his fist. "Curse those Parliament troops! First they desecrate Canterbury Cathedral, riding their horses down the aisles to shatter stained glass and destroy the altars. Then up north they murder peasants taking refuge in the village church."

The messenger's face whitened. "Beg your pardon, sire. It was no Parliament troops did this in Cheshire. 'Twas our own."

The King jumped to his feet, a vein standing out purple on his neck. "A loyal supporter of mine dares to commit this folly?"

"Nay, your Majesty." The courier bowed low in fear. "The commander was visiting his wife and newborn daughter a long ride away, when an unorthodox landowner stirred up the troops."

"His name?"

"Dryden Scudamore."

"We have heard of the fellow. He hath not much fear of God, and already a shadow taints his name."

Sir Robert clenched his hands on his lap, then uncon-

Part II: Honour

sciously felt for the weapon hilt on his hip. *I know the man*, he thought, but kept his lips still.

"We shall send word to the Church authorities and watch this renegade carefully."

"May I be assigned the task?" Sir Robert asked.

The King shook his hair against the lace collar. "Nay. Though we know you desire to inspect your own holdings and family, we have greater need of you elsewhere. The Scots are a treacherous lot, moving back and forth across the borders to Newcastle. And down in Kent, the nobles near Maidstone continue to plague us with their endless petitions."

The King sighed and picked up his goblet, while Sir Edmund Verney studied his friend Robert. He seemed hard-put to control his agitation over the turn of events near home.

* * *

Within two weeks, the Stafford Town Council assembled hastily at an inn in southern Staffordshire. It was early morning.

William Comberford, clad in his best leather doublet, rose from the table. He gestured for the clerk to report.

"As ye are already aware, last evening word came of the King's approach toward our town." The clerk paused and brushed a speck of soil from his simple black garments. "His Majesty gathers an army to stand against Parliament, and he comes to garner our support. Despite slow progress on the narrow road, arrival is imminent, and..."

An elderly councilman interrupted. "What be our chances of remaining neutral in this—this festering conflict?"

Comberford looked round the table and leaned forward. "Since we have raised no neutral army, it appears we shall be forced to choose sides."

The clerk nodded his short-cropped head. "Yet a traveler told me the landowners at Uttoxeter chose not to join with the King. His Majesty raised no troops there, though I cannot fathom how the gentry slithered out of it."

Richard Sneade swept his decorated sleeve across the assembly. "Dare we defy our sovereign, as he encamps but a day or two from our doorsteps?" His words were sharp, and the sash across his chest heaved with indignation.

Comberford reached for the document in the clerk's hands. "Gentlemen, hear this received only today's morn:

> *To the good men of Stafford,*
> *Herein find an order for 10,000 pennyworth of*
> *bread to be ready next day.*
> *Signed,*
> *Mr. Leonard Picknay*
> *His Majesty's Commissary*

Another member of the gentry half rose from the bench. "We haven't bread enough in the entire town to feed an army. At Nottingham, I am told, 800 soldiers of horse and 300 of foot raised the standard with the King. And, despite the Uttoxeter response, the numbers surely are swelling."

William Comberford nodded. "I could send John Clarke to Penkrich and Wolverhampton to order bread, and a messenger to Lichfield as well." He looked at Richard Sneade. "Might Elizabeth Jones have fresh rushes to make ready for His Majesty's way to the church?"

"Yes." The ruff at Sneade's throat vibrated as he swallowed. "I personally commit myself to the royal effort. And I am prepared to extend the hospitality of High House to King Charles, the Prince, and their advisors. My allegiance belongs to my sovereign. The rest of the troops shall have to find quarter among the townsfolk wherever they can."

Comberford looked steadily around the table, eye-to-eye

Part II: Honour

with each man present. "Is this to be Stafford's agreed response? To embrace the King's army and thus repudiate Parliament?"

"If thus, let us pray it shall be the prevailing side." The clerk scraped his stool. "'Tis said the troops grumbled much as they passed Chartley, for His Majesty refused to let them pillage the estate."

One of the gentry smacked his heel against the floor. "The Earl of Essex should consider himself fortunate. Imagine the King ignoring the opportunity to strike at property of Parliament's commander-in-chief!"

The old man turned to Comberford, with a thoughtful expression on his face. "Does that make His Majesty weak, indecisive, or a gentleman cut from finer cloth than the Roundheads?"

The youngest at the table responded. "Whatever we think, an angry king at the town gate is more threat than hordes of Puritans concentrated in London."

The councillors nodded in agreement.

Sneade added, "Let us alert the local militia and choose additional bodyguards for the King for the duration of his stay in our county."

Comberford slapped the edge of the table. "Then it is decided. I urge that if His Majesty proceeds to Stafford—and it appears so—he shall have access to it and have the best entertainment the troublesome times afford!"

"Hear! Hear!" the council chorused, then they adjourned.

* * *

By afternoon an advance party from the King arrived in Stafford. With them came acceptance of hospitality at High House. Richard Sneade and his wife Grace had already issued a sudden flurry of orders to their household staff in preparation for the most important guest since the house was built. All four floors were to be scoured, food for sumptuous feasting was ordered, and nothing but the finest furnishings remained in the largest chamber. The rambling half-timbered home on Greengate Street became a blur of activity.

Among the royal advance party was Ralph Sneade. A clean-shaven man with curling hair, Ralph rushed through the front doors to greet Richard, the master of High House. "I am to be made a colonel two days hence—and by His Majesty's own hand in thine house! What sayest thou to this, younger brother?"

Richard clapped his sibling on the back and drew him into the study. "Splendid! I understand by courier that I am to be a captain myself. May your distinguished rank help the cause and, I pray, gain the ear of the King. Loyalties are uncertain up north and we must see that our relatives and neighbours are better protected. This visit shall cost me a small fortune, yet perhaps in another way it will pay well. Will you aid me in persuading the King to send a suitable leader there, Ralph? Thy colonel's rank, coupled with this mere captain's, should wield some influence."

"Yea, I shall happily help you. Let us ask the King's standard bearers for the name of a competent soldier equal to the task. Naming the man is first step to the deed being accomplished."

On the 17th of September, the King and his army entered the East Gate, greeted by the town dignitaries. The citizens of Stafford leaned out their windows for a view of King Charles and his sizable entourage. Sir Edmund Verney and Sir Robert Mayfield, in the cavalry regalia of the Lifeguards, bore the royal standards down Greengate Street toward High House. One of the painted taffeta colors, emblazoned with a crowned lion, boldly proclaimed the motto, "Ready with either weapon."

While the King set up Court in the finest bedchamber of

Part II: Honour

the house, Richard Sneade drew Verney and Mayfield into the study for stout refreshment. Ralph waited there, eager for the latest reports.

Sir Edmund Verney tapped his boot wearily on the woven mat flooring. "Rumors abound that some Roundhead regiments are moving up from London, establishing a garrison at Newcastle-under-Lyme. Way to the north, the Scots grumble continually over the prayerbook. The king is sorely pressed on many sides."

Ralph Sneade straightened in his chair. "Is there not trouble with the Treasury as well? His Majesty's coffers are seeing bottom, so he prepares to force more loans and confiscate more lands. Let us hope he leaves our holdings alone and takes only the Parliamentarians' assets."

Sir Mayfield cleared his throat. "I fear he cannot recompense his subjects—or the various regiments—as promised. Furthermore, discontent over billeting soldiers shall only intensify. This business of the cavalry living at free quarter..." He lowered his voice. "Scavenging whatever they can get around the countryside....Well, it works to the detriment of my own family and lands even this day—and threatens the King's cause among even the noblest supporters."

Ralph leaned toward Mayfield and chose his words carefully. "But hear me in this view. The corner of northern Staffordshire, nigh unto your estate, is a pocket of vulnerability, from both directions. Help us persuade His Majesty to move in a small second force to the area. If Dryden Scudamore's estate has no further room for billeting, as I suspect, your household could be well served. A nuisance becomes extra protection."

"You speak wisely." He lowered his voice. "Dryden himself bears watching. You have no doubt heard of his exploits up in Cheshire. Then there's the situation with those unpredictable Scots raiding back and forth across the border. The Earl of Essex is now proclaimed a traitor to the realm. And the Parliamentarians may push north after their rampage at Canterbury." He shook his head, recalling the assault on the majestic cathedral and Thomas a' Becket's shrine. "They stop at nothing. Our families need more protection, even if we sacrifice wealth in the bargain."

Edmund Verney spoke thoughtfully. "His Majesty may be convinced to divert a contingent enroute to join us—if he feels assured the Oxford road will be well enough guarded. From my recent visit home to Aylesbury, I judge my lands secure enough for now. The King continues to raise support as he moves toward Shrewsbury. Perhaps another regiment could be spared for your corner of Staffordshire. And I know the man, a one Richard Allen of York.

"But is he not the commander newly promoted?" asked Mayfield.

"Indeed, he is, and handling his troops of horse capably."

Ralph leaned forward. "Did not his father serve against the Irish just months ago?"

"And gave his life valiantly. No question," Verney responded. "This second son is a less tried man in battle, but possesses unerring character."

"How so?" Mayfield asked.

"He came to soldiering from priestly studies, if memory serves me well. More fit to be a scholar than a captain, perhaps, but worthy of trust..."

Mayfield thought of Catherine and Honour. "Even with one's wife and daughter?"

Verney nodded. "Allen is a just and courageous man."

"Then let us approach the King about it at eventide."

* * *

Early the next morning, two upstairs maids passed by a leaded window.

Part II: Honour

Katie, the younger servant new to High House, stopped abruptly. "It's him!"

"Careful! You most nearly dropped the whole stack of bedlinen, all clean and pressed."

"But, Peg, 'tis the Prince. I been hoping for days now to get a glimpse of him." Her cap bobbed with enthusiasm. "Ever since we heared they was comin'."

"Hrumpf. Makes a lot more work for our kind and costs the master a fair fortune."

Katie propped the bedding against the older woman's ample bosom. "You've heard the same tales as me. Such a brave fighter from the Continent!" She opened the window wider, leaned out, and pointed toward the garden. "Isn't he the most dashing man you ever seen?"

On the walkway below stood the King with his nephew, their host Richard Sneade, and several advisors. Prince Rupert of the Rhine, at twenty-three years, bore a striking resemblance to England's older Sovereign. Loose brown curls touched Rupert's shoulders. Smooth brows arched over heavy-lidded eyes. But, unlike his relative, the younger man's full lips turned upward at the corners.

The Prince wrinkled his aristocratic nose as he engaged in good-natured banter with the others. The feather in his hat danced when he laughed.

King Charles placed a fingertip against his bearded chin, as he leaned thoughtfully toward his clean-shaven nephew. "Word has it you make a fine shot with that horseman's pistol of yours. But since the standard went up at Nottingham, I've not had a proper demonstration."

The advisors in the garden looked one to another.

"Then, Uncle, you shall have it now." Rupert withdrew his sack of powder and briskly loaded the pistol with its single bullet. He looked round for a worthy target.

Richard Sneade gestured toward the Church of St. Mary's. "'Tis a full sixty yards to yonder steeple. Think you can hit the weathercock upon it?"

"A clever choice of target, Captain Sneade." The King looked smug as he challenged Rupert. "'Tis a small one, and far."

Rupert's face came alive with humor and he scraped an exaggerated bow. "It's just right, Your Majesty." He straightened and resumed a military bearing. The Prince raised his pistol, sighted the target, and fired.

Ping!

The master of the house and his guests chuckled among themselves. For the bullet had pierced the weathercock's tail, and daylight shone straight through.

"Well, well." The King clapped his nephew on the shoulder. "You're a lucky man—today."

The Rhine Prince grinned and reloaded his piece. He aimed and fired, again.

Ping! A distinct second hole gaped in the tail of the metal rooster. All in the garden but Charles applauded.

Rupert turned to the King with a bit of a smirk. "Luck or talent, Your Majesty. You choose." He put away his weapon and slowly donned his gloves.

Charles fingered his wispy mustache. "Your skill appears to match your reputation, at least in this instance." The King conceded a tight smile to his nephew and started to walk away.

Three paces down the path, the royal cloak swung round. A solemn face addressed Prince Rupert. "By the way, I'll need you to depart before us. As Commander of Horse, begin to move the cavalry tomorrow toward Worcester."

Rupert nodded. "Of course. And I thank you, Uncle, for issuing my orders directly—not through an underling."

Three storeys above the garden, Katie closed the window and turned to Peg. "Didn't I tell you?"

Chapter Ten

※

*W*ithout fanfare, the band of cavalry troopers moved upcountry, hampered by muddy roads and the poor condition of their horses. Not one estate they passed could improve their lot.

By the time the soldiers reached Keele village, their commander's dragoon pony suffered lameness and moved as one nearly dead on the hoof. A pan of oats at the inn had bribed the beast as far as the manor. But when Richard Allen dismounted just inside the cobblestone courtyard, the animal went down.

The tall captain with Viking features gestured to his second in command, who was also his trusted friend. "Edward, gather some men to drag it outside the wall—and be mercifully quick rendering its fate. I shall report at once to the senior officer here."

* * *

Within the mighty sandstone house, Lady Catherine interrupted her descent on the grand staircase. Her step paused at the landing. *What new commotion strikes the courtyard this day?*

She peered out the window even with the landing, beneath the scythe and *fleur-de-lis* in new stained glass, a tribute to her ancestry. *Another contingent to sleep and feed, no doubt. I'd best alert the housekeeper.*

First, she said a prayer for her husband's safe return.

* * *

Honour looked up at last. Her head ached, and holding the quill so long had stiffened the muscles in her hand. But on the table before her lay the beginnings of a journal, blots and all, and a completed missive ready for courier to her father.

She smiled, knowing few soldiers, even among the King's standard bearers, could boast a daughter literate as she. Her heart warmed as she imagined his joy at receiving the letter.

But the gaping hole left by his departure lingered.

She pushed back the chair and wandered to the leaded window. The new band of Cavaliers loitered on the cobblestones below. One stood apart from the others, his broad back to her. She caught a glimpse of wild light hair and wondered idly to whom it belonged. *Time enough, and I shall see his face.* Sooner or later, they all made a weak excuse to glimpse her dark tresses and creamy skin. Mirth bubbled up, catching her off-guard. *Will this stranger stumble all over himself like the others?*

Honour turned from the window and reached for her sealing wax.

* * *

Down in the courtyard, the Cavalier recalled his most important duty of the day. He approached a liveried servant

Part II: Honour

at the main door. "Which way to the stables?"

* * *

"With all due respect, sire, the young mistress shan't like it." Jack, a Mayfield groom, shifted from one foot to another, still holding tight the tether. "She puts great store in this Barbary mare."

"'Tis finely bred, indeed. And tall. Perfect for a cavalry horse. Just inform the girl she has no say in the matter. The poor pony that brought me collapsed at the gate. I must have a mount, else my men and I cannot help guard this place. I am under King's orders."

The newcomer grasped the bridle and reached into the manger for a fistful of hay. "What do they call her?"

"Lady Honour."

He sighed in frustration. "No, I mean the horse."

"Beg pardon, sire. It be Snowflake, on account of her face."

The soldier stroked the animal's white star. "From this day until I release her, this battle-worthy animal is to be for my use alone."

* * *

Jack sent word for Honour's personal maid, who was also his wife, to meet him behind the main kitchens. As Molly passed outside the door, he pulled her into the shadows and stole a kiss.

"Aye, so what be your excuse this day to call me outside?" Dimples in her cheeks gave away her pleasure, before she hid her face coyly in her apron.

He smiled but grew straight-faced again. "'Tis some real trouble, I fear, for your young lady."

Molly gave him a puzzled look.

"The captain of yonder soldiering unit put down his nag on arrival and takes a fancy to that blaze-faced steed."

Molly clapped her hand to her mouth. "Surely not milady's Snowflake?"

Jack nodded. "The same, and more. He claims the mare for his own, forbidding any other to ride her."

"Trouble you can say thrice." Molly shook her capped head. "The girl shall raise the chimneys off the house over that piece of horseflesh. 'Tis the gift of her father."

"Yea, Molly. Methinks you must be the one to tell her, easy."

Molly stamped her foot. "'Tis a dirty job you put on my head, Jack. But for God's peace, better I tell her than another."

"Good girl." He patted her bottom lightly as she scooted away. "Best you do it before sundown."

Chapter Eleven

*L*oud, urgent hoofbeats shattered the early morning quiet.

Honour rose quickly from her mirror, her heavy braid left unfinished. She ran to the window and pressed her face to the glass. A youth in her father's livery ducked into the servants' entrance, not even taking care to tie up the lathered black horse. Sides still heaving, it pawed the cobblestones with its hooves.

"Oh, Molly, it must be news of Father! Hurry down the back stairs. Pray listen to what news he brings. It is much too long since he hath writ a letter!"

Abruptly, Honour tied a loose ribbon where the braid's end should have been, rushed to finish dressing, and glided slim feet into kid slippers. As she reached for the door, it opened from the hallway.

"Oh, Miss!" Molly faced her with lines of fear newly etched in her young face. "The mistress wants to see you in the library right now."

The girls' eyes met for an instant. Honour took a deep breath, lifted her hem, and ran down the grand staircase, barely brushing the stair carpet as she went. At the foot of the stairs, she plunged down the hallway to the right and entered the library, a place she often fled for sanctuary from the troops stomping through the house.

This autumn morning the rich dark wood paneling was gilded by rare sunshine. Light seemed to dance on the white marble fireplace as brilliance from the fish pond streamed in the tall arched windows. A small but revered collection of books lay on a table in the center of the room.

Honour's mother stood woodenly before the fire. She stared into the flames. Catherine's back faced the door, once-straight shoulders hunched. One trembling hand held the letter. From the other dangled a scarlet battle scarf.

Honour felt something deep inside her plummet. Slowly, Honour crossed the distance to her mother and slid between her and the hearth. A sense of foreboding enveloped her as a cloud.

"Mother," she whispered. Honour's eyes finally looked from the shaking hand into her dear mother's face. Involuntarily, Honour's hand flew to her own mouth.

All vitality had drained from the familiar face, leaving only a gray pallor. The raised scarf flamed against her cheek.

When Catherine met the look of her only daughter, her features flashed despair. She crumpled into sobs, and Honour reached for her, offering support.

"Oh, Mother. "'Tis—'tis Father, is it not?" She paused, almost daring not to breathe.

Then questions rushed. "Is he wounded in battle? Or the King's guard captured?" She touched the silken emblem of her father's loyalty and felt the stiffness of blood. Her heart faltered.

Catherine looked up at her daughter, so full of life and promise, and shook her head. Tears brimmed in her eyes and voice. "No, Honour, your father has fallen. God save us all. He is—dead." She clutched at Honour to keep her balance.

The girl reached into her silken sleeve for a cloth. She tenderly dabbed at her mother's tears as her own welled up. "Who—who sent the missive?"

"Sir Sydenham. Here, read it to me. I could only understand parts of it."

As she reached for the message, Honour remembered the precious times she and her father had shared, hunched over a candle in this very room. He had taught her to read from the recently translated English Bible, ordered by James I, the present monarch's father.

Honour blinked away a tear, and tried to steady her voice. Even so, she read haltingly, breathlessly.

> *My dear Mistress Mayfield—*
>
> *It grieves me sorely to bring you this word.*
>
> *On this 23 October, the King's regiments clashed with the Earl of Essex' forces in a brutal battle at Edgehill. Afterward 5000 Englishmen lay dead. An extreme struggle against Sir William Constable's Regiments of Foot ensued around the royal standard. Sir Robert breathed his last defending the noble banner, and fell beside Knight Marshal Sir Edmund Verney. The life of the Sovereign is preserved at their sacrifice. May your grieving household be proud, knowing Sir Robert was a man of courage and faithfulness.*
>
> *It was needful to bury Sir Mayfield at once near Kineton for fear of the plague. The Vicar of Kineton and I attended to your husband's remains personally.*
>
> *May God in His infinite mercy comfort you.*
> *Signed,*
> *Sir Edward Sydenham*
> *28 October, the year of our Lord 1642*

Catherine choked, "We must get word somehow to Andrew on the Continent, but I know not even where he is. It could take months." She hesitated. "We must, then, send a messenger to Dryden. I shall have to rely on his counsel instead."

Honour felt a momentary stab of fear. "Could we not manage the lands as we are doing until my brother returns?" She almost continued aloud, but bit back the thought, *Dryden is not a man like unto my father*. A shudder passed through her as she remembered how Dryden once forced her onto his lap, slipping his hands up her skirt. And she little more than a child at the time.

Catherine shook her head slowly. "He is our nearest neighbour. We have not much choice. Our lands adjoin and our families are much connected. We must depend on him to advise us."

"Father taught me much. I can read most of the documents needful."

"Yet, we must have the security of a protector, a—a man. Surely, you must see that, my daughter."

"But can you trust him?" Honour knew for herself it was impossible.

Catherine smiled wanly and reached out her hand for the letter. "We must. I know you have never felt warmly toward him, but he is all we have at present." Her glance fell again upon the terrible words in her hand. She ran her fingers over the scarf in a final loving gesture.

Catherine erupted in fresh sobs and fled the room.

Honour dragged her slippered feet toward the bright windows. She blinked as the light caught her tear-damp lashes.

How can any heart be rent in twain on such a glorious day as this? Her gaze reached past the awakening garden and hedgerows and rested on the tree-studded meadow on the hill. *The hill.* Her heart sank at the thought. Just over that

Part II: Honour

rise lay the manor of her future guardian.

Oh, dear God, save me from him. Father... A fresh rush of tears overtook Honour, as she realized anew the loss of her loving protector.

A soft shuffling sound in the far corner interrupted her thoughts. Honour whirled from the window. "Who..." Her eyes narrowed to adapt to the dimness of the library.

From behind the delicately painted screen, a man's form appeared, hands outstretched, palms turned up.

As her eyes adjusted to the oaken room, Honour gasped. "Who are you! What are you doing here? Listening all the while!" she choked. Using her hand as a shield, she rushed toward the door.

The commanding man nimbly stepped forward, placing a firm grip on her arm. The sheaf of his sword clinked as he lowered the taut hand from her face and turned her toward himself.

In a rush of indignation, Honour gave the soldier a scathing close inspection. Because of his Viking height, her eyes met his bearded chin first. When they lowered to the breadth of his shoulders, recognition dawned. *The soldier of the courtyard.*

Reddish whiskers parted for a well-shaped mouth. "Please, please Miss Mayfield. I did not intend..."

She tried to wiggle free, looking down where his fingers still clasped her arm. From there her inspection dropped to his striped knee-length trousers. Mud crusted the tall doeskin boots he wore.

"Hear me! God's truth, I had a wearisome night at sentry duty and was still restless when allowed to sleep early this morn. Books bring great comfort to me, and I merely came here to find a volume of your father's to settle my mind. Sleep overtook me on the couch."

She searched his face. His light hair was mashed down on top, where his plumed hat had been, and the long curly sides looked badly tousled. Surely there were tired lines around his keen blue eyes.

"Indeed, I had no plan to spy on you and the mistress—even less so at such a time."

Those eyes. Midnight blue framed with red-gold lashes.

He met her inspection boldly, without blinking or looking away.

Earnest eyes. She nearly voiced the thought. "Ah—I believe you. But—my beloved father—dead!"

He reached his other arm toward her. The man ventured a response, his voice quiet, rich-timbred with feeling. "I know that pain as well. My own father fell in the Irish Rebellion not one year since, and—I know not even where they buried him."

At her startled look, the soldier eased his grip on Honour's hands. His touch traveled up the delicate folds of her sleeves. And his gaze rested briefly on her velvet bodice before returning to her face. A muscle worked in his thick neck.

"I am a military man. My word to my king pledges to him my life. Yet this new flow of human blood on our country's fields sickens me. What times we live in! Trusted friends become traitors. Sons battle against fathers. King and subjects seek to murder one another. All the kingdom is in pain!"

Honour's eyes widened at the vehemence of his statements. Hardly realizing she was dropping her guard, she blurted, "Oh, sir, great fear gnaws within me for my family. Our near neighbour has designs on our lands, and his..." She paused, trying to shut out the memory of leering eyes. "He frightens me."

He felt a tremor go through her body.

"My mother thinks him trustworthy. But I—never!" Honour swayed slightly toward the captain's tunic and sash.

A shaft of sunlight caught the blue-black luster of

Honour's tresses. Instinctively, the captain touched the ribbon binding her heavy braid. In doing so, his wide fingers accidently brushed past a fluff of lace and met creamy skin.

He drew the hand away quickly, as if to stop a burn. Honour's heart beat wildly. She cast down her eyes in confusion. Never before had she felt such a rush of attraction to any man.

As the blond intruder spoke, she pulled her attention back to his words. "Might you perchance trust me, lovely Honour? Though it may rankle your family to have our troops billeted these weeks, our presence here may give your neighbour pause. And allow time for wise counsel."

He tossed his head abruptly and placed both hands on her shoulders, his thumbs on her collarbone. She was forced to look right into his face. "Before God, I swear to allow no harm to come to you. From this day on, I would protect you with my life."

His eyes blazed with unusual light, and Honour found herself unable to look away. She mused aloud, "You pledge me your life, and I know not even your name."

"Captain Allen. Richard Allen, second son of the Earl of Howard—God rest his soul." He paused while she absorbed his words. "Can you find in your heart some belief in me?"

In a sudden flash, Honour awoke as if from a trance. "Trust you? The one my groom witnessed taking for yourself Father's last gift, Snowflake. How dare you make promises of concern, with mud still on your boots from riding sentry—on my own horse this night past!"

She ripped away from his touch and put her hands against the sides of her face. "No!" she screamed. "Never, as long as I live!"

Honour flung out her arms and spun on one heel for the door. So violently did she turn, that she struck a vase of Michaelmas daisies on a nearby table. The blossoms crashed to the floor as she fled upstairs.

Chapter Twelve

Sheet lightning lit up the entire plain. Dryden Scudamore reigned in his horse tightly where a narrow track led to the right. He started to turn the beast toward the little-used shortcut.

An involuntary shiver crawled up his neck. For a moment, he weighed the forbidding path again.

"Bah! Talk of haunts on this Mayfield land is naught to me." His voice sounded overloud in his own ears.

As one, aristocrat and mount plunged toward the mantle of dense branches, lured by a promised respite from the near-drenching to come.

Riding boots dug into the horse's flanks. Dryden's ill-matched eyes—one green and one brown—flicked upward as he rode. Nature's ceiling blackened overhead.

Those ignorant peasants imagined to hold out on the full rents due me. He jingled the purse at his thigh. *But I bested them—yet another year!*

Thin lips curled in perverse pleasure, while the lone horseman reached for the whip and snapped it triumphantly across the animal's rump.

Another low rumble chased across the sky. Dryden's

face creased and the corners of his mouth turned down. *'Twere not for their greed, I should be in my library, relishing both coin and fireside. Curse their stingy hides!*

In the depths of the valley, Dryden leaned close to the equine neck. A scowl that matched the sky creviced his face. "Deliver me to the stable before the deluge—or want for the oats tonight."

A sudden spatter of raindrops peppered Dryden's broad hat. Its feather twitched in the gust, and stringy gray hair whipped into Dryden's eyes. "God's blood," he muttered, and freed a hand from the reins to reset the hat.

At that moment, the sky split with a river of lightning. Dryden's mount reared, pawing at the charged air. The man clutched at the reins with his remaining hand, but it was not enough.

In the blinding flash, Dryden seemed suspended, then tipped backward from the saddle and his elegant boots slipped unevenly from the stirrups. In the increasing downpour, he thudded to the earth.

The horse ran on, fueled by fear and confusion.

Throughout the long night, the nobleman lay where he fell. Not one soul of consequence at the manor even missed him.

* * *

Near dawn he awoke and tried to move. A dart of pain lanced the left leg. As Dryden lifted his head, a rivulet of cold rain traced down his neck. His lace ruff was soaked, and even the leather jerkin, nearly wet through. A chill vibrated his leg. He howled in pain.

"The—knee," he gritted through his rotting teeth, "must be—out of joint."

He lay back down, sweating. *No travelers, nay, even robbers, dare this track. I am all I have.*

Part II: Honour

Thus it has always been, thought Dryden as he lay there. Unwelcome in the Scudamore family as a bad omen, suspect among the peerage for his evil eyes. *But I wrested my portion—and my brother's—even so. I did it on my own. All I rule is by my making, and I dare not lose it now...to this.* He looked in disgust at the at the twisted limb.

The tarnished man gathered his strength and dragged his ponderous form to the nearest tree trunk. Breathing heavily, he felt the goose lump on the back of his head. It throbbed yet.

"Where went that confounded horse?" He whistled. Silence. A yawning quiet filled the wood. No hoof fall, no warm breath.

"Gone." Through the trees came the first telltale signs of day. He groped in the semi-darkness and reached an isolated piece of leather, broken in the fall. "Aha!" Faster, his hands searched, revealing splintered wood from the saddle.

After fashioning a crude splint, Dryden dragged himself along the leafmold floor nearly a rapier length, then collapsed. The off-color eyes winced, then bulged at the added effort. Cradling the injured limb, the man turned his head round.

A cry of ecstasy mingled with the misery on his lips. No more than a few horse gaits away, bare trees revealed an opening in the hill. Rejuvenated at the thought of shelter, Dryden heaved a great effort, and dragged himself through the brush to the cave.

As he struggled upright, a shaft of dawn's rays spilled into the lair. *An argent gleam!* He peered closer, all muscles tensed. The man's pulses raced.

"Sweet mammon! Can it be for certain?" Heedless of pain, he pushed closer. Practiced fingertips discerned the silver vein.

Dank cold left his body and a feverish glow lit at his core. "I must make it mine. Mine. All mine!"

Chapter Thirteen

"Peddler coming! Peddler on Mayfield lands!" The joyful cry rang quickly throughout the residents of the Hall, nobles and servants alike.

But Honour was nowhere in evidence. Perplexed, Molly searched the main wings. "Where is the young mistress? She cannot miss the peddler. 'Twon't be back for months!"

An older maid Jane, laden with clean linen, offered, "Might she be out riding? 'Tis a fine day."

"No more, not since that mud-trailing soldier took her horse for himself." Molly's eyes darkened as she lowered her voice. "His kind brings more trouble than safety, I am thinking."

"Washing, aplenty, that is sure!" Her gap-toothed smile was wide.

"More than that! Why, Jack tells me—keep it private, you will—only two nights ago mating noises came loud through the barn walls, and it was no cattle either!"

"Who's sure if it's soldiers or not. I hear tell that foul-mouthed dairyman won't leave poor Fanny alone. And with me own eyes, I saw the young mistress cleaning cuts and salving bruises on that unfortunate little mite." The

Circle of Love

washwoman shifted her load, then trudged on.

Molly muttered to herself. "Soldiers and that snake—two more reasons to find Honour now."

Room after room turned up no sign of her. *There is another place*, she thought. At once, Molly climbed to the minstrel balcony overlooking the Great Hall, and approached the room atop the main entrance. An unornamented door stood slightly ajar. She rapped loudly and entered.

"At last, my lady, here you are!" Molly wiped her brow with an apron corner.

Honour only half turned from the curved glass window. Her hand still rested on the curtain, which fluttered slightly in the autumn breeze.

"Pray, come with me to the courtyard. The peddler nears the gate!"

"I can see and hear for myself. But I need nothing. Baubles and trinkets interest me not today."

"Nor other days. Yet before your father left..."

Honour whirred fully around. Molly saw sadness in her lady's visage, but she pressed, "...a pair of horses could not prevent your viewing the wares."

"Before he left home, to run after the King's enemies, I cared about many things. But now..."

The servant tentatively stretched out her hand. "He is gone, and much is different."

Honour nodded, unable to speak.

Molly looked around the room and saw the girl's journal lying there. "This place. 'Tis where you saw him last."

"Almost nightly in my dreams, I stand at this window waving. Always he rides proudly out the gate—to die."

"For all his loyalty to the King, methinks he loved you more." Molly stepped closer to the window, her headdress bobbing in certainty. "Yea, much more."

The servant's expression altered suddenly. She hopped

Part II: Honour

on one foot and pointed. "Hark! He comes through the gate!" She urged, "Do come! News of the King's fortunes he may also bring."

Honour's lips curved ever so slightly. "Well, all right. I shall go with you this once."

Molly sprang toward the gallery.

* * *

Honour started to follow, when a certain movement in the chaos of the courtyard captured her attention. A masculine form—so tall he now hid the bent peddler—lifted his head toward the house, indeed, the very window where Honour stood. She sucked in her breath.

The Cavalier removed his broad plumed hat, acknowledging the lady's frown with a exaggerated, comical bow. His boots clicked on the cobbles. Straw-colored hair tumbled to wide shoulders and covered some of the immaculate lace around his throat. The crooked smile on his lips faded suddenly. From beneath brows that shone white in the sun, his eyes sought hers. For only the briefest instant, they latched.

A flash of feeling vaulted in Honour's breast. She looked away, but could not withstand a second tempting glance. His eyes still sought her visage. She whirled toward the door and caught the toe of her slipper on a chair. Grateful that Molly had led the way downstairs, Honour touched a fingertip to the pink confusion that lay naked on her face. She took her time descending the stairs.

The peddler at the center of the melee spread out his wares, gesturing wildly, and pocketed coin after coin. A dense crowd surged around him.

Someone asked, "What news bring ye?"

The peddler paused in his selling. "His Majesty entered Oxford only six days after the blood-letting at Edgehill. And

Circle of Love

he sends troops toward Reading. Rumor has it Prince Rupert plundered Broughton Castle nigh Banbury but cannot break the Parliament forces defending Windsor. London is seething over the Prince's action."

Murmurs circled the crowd as the seller returned to his occupation.

Molly leaned over him from the side opposite her lady.

The grizzled old hawker opened a soft cloth. Its contents sparkled in the sun. The maid pointed for her lady to look.

Curiosity awoke in Honour and she leaned in closer. Seeing her noble bearing, the peddler dropped the round medallion into her outstretched hand.

"'Tis unusually fine craftsmanship. From whence does it come?"

"Far down the road, only a day out of London. The maker will stutter to his death, but his work would grace your neck finely. You'll not have another chance to buy for many months."

Her fingertips traced the delicate flowers and vines, then replaced the piece in the cloth. "I have not the heart for it today."

Just then an errant elbow jabbed Honour in the ribs and someone else trounced her dainty feet. She turned wearily toward the house when the crowd pressed her against a solid wall of muscle.

"Good day, milady." The soldier inclined his head, one hand lifting the hat, while the other stroked his beard. Replaced atop his curls, the hat shaded his expression.

"Captain Allen." She kept her greeting civil though cool, but her voice felt shaky. "You mock me."

He guided her toward the edge of the crowd, then leaned closer and placed a hand on her elbow. "Your disapproval breaks my heart," he whispered. As he smiled, his mustache lightly grazed her ear.

Honour stiffened. "'Twas you who took my horse!"

"Granted. But ponder this. Care you nothing for the protection my soldiers and the Mayfield horseflesh afford you, together?" The pressure of his fingers on her arm increased.

Her cheeks flushed. "I wish to have Snowflake in my personal care."

"She is tended well." The defense sounded more like a caress.

"Would that I knew it."

The Cavalier's touch wandered to the young woman's waist. As his thumb idly grazed her rib, she found herself lulled temporarily by his courtliness. And the new pleasure of his gentle ways.

"Indeed. Perhaps you should prove it to yourself. Come and see."

Honour's chin lifted. "Very well. Where is she?"

"This way, milady."

He guided her deftly around the stragglers and through the courtyard gate. Beyond the stone portals, rolling hills stood lush and green from recent rains. And lavender Michaelmas daisies still bloomed, scattered through the lightly wooded area before them.

The soldier and girl turned into the bridle path that encircled the manor house. He dropped his hand from her elbow and drew his rapier from its sheath. She stopped midstride, a quizzical expression on her face.

"A mere precaution. But one must be careful in these unsettled days." *Nights, as well*, he added to himself, as they resumed their pace.

The two had not strolled far when Honour came upon Snowflake tethered to an oak tree. A nicker of recognition met her outstretched hand.

"Snowflake, I miss you so." Practiced fingers smoothed the sleek coat, touching the starred face with familiarity. Then Honour stepped back and surveyed her special charge, first from one side, then another, all the way round.

She bent to inspect a hoof. "Does the soldier pace you hard, day and night?"

Richard tilted his headpiece and approached the horse. He withdrew a misshapen carrot from his pocket. "I abuse you greatly, do I not, my friend?" Tiny lines at the corners of his eyes gave his mirth away.

"I concede you have not harmed her—yet."

"Truce?" His face lit with the question.

She delayed her answer, comparing this man with her father.

"A peace offering, then?" Ignoring her silence, he strode off the path toward a clump of autumn daisies. With his weapon, Captain Allen cut a modest bouquet and returned to Honour's side.

With a boyish grin across his face, he thrust the flowers into her hands and brushed his mustache against her cheek. The fleeting kiss came light as a butterfly.

The awareness of his touch, aye, even his momentary glance at the window, besieged her. But she resolved it was not enough. Quickly, lest she weaken, Honour dropped the fragile blooms on the path between them.

Her brows furrowed and creamy chin jutted upward. Unshed tears balanced precariously against her lashes. Her nails bit into the palms of her hands. The girl-woman gulped for words. "How can—you—cherish Snowflake as I myself? The moment you spill her blood in battle, you take—my—my father's final gift from me as well."

A twig snapped underfoot when she turned, and she was gone.

Richard stared at the truce scattered at his feet.

* * *

A single blossom had caught in Honour's heavy skirts.

Part II: Honour

Upstairs in her room, when the bruised bud fell onto the floor, she picked it up tenderly, pressed it to her breast, and let the tears flow.

Later, she touched her cheek and remembered Richard's kiss.

Chapter Fourteen

Dryden lowered himself gingerly into the drawing room chair. He absentmindedly caressed the injured knee, while he spoke in honeyed tones.

"Ah, but dearest Catherine, you know I have her best interests at heart. Have I not guided you wisely these days since your precious Robert deceased?"

The lady twisted her ring, her eyes lowered. "I—I had thought Honour might wish a match closer to her own age, such as Robert and I were. And the thought of her leaving Mayfield Manor..." Catherine sighed. "Though many marry younger, she is barely seventeen, and I would miss her."

"It is time to get on with the marriage. Our lands adjoin. Aught but a carriage ride away, 'twould be. Besides, the advantages I could give her weigh heavily." He worked hard to hold back his sense of urgency, not adverse to certain advantages of his own. "And your, ah, debts..." He feigned a reluctant expression.

She looked him square in the eyes. "Verily, I know. You need not remind me of them." A sharp edge had crept into her voice, and she wondered what it was about this man that bothered her in these recent days. "Widow's nerves."

Circle of Love

Dryden's straight eyebrows rose. "Pardon?"

"I—You speak of the debts again. Is there no other way to handle them and keep my daughter in this house yet awhile longer?"

The landowner rose slowly from his chair and lifted Catherine's smooth face toward his. "Well." He hesitated ever so briefly. "You could marry me. I am but a few years younger than you." His fingertips crabbed slowly along her cheek. "You are still a desirable woman."

Abruptly, she turned her head aside. "At present, I cannot conceive of marrying again. Perhaps I never shall."

His fingers, still on her face, tightened. "Very well. I shall consider that subject closed." His hand fell to his side. "But you must speak to Honour about her duty to the family—soon."

The prospective bridegroom picked up his cane and limped from the room.

Catherine stared out the arched window. Then bowed her head. *Oh, Robert, I feel so alone.*

* * *

Dryden fingered the ring in his hand and glanced up sharply at his steward. "The village smith hath done merely a tolerable work."

"He said 'twas best he could make in the scarce time allotted."

The landowner limped to the window. The jewelry between his claws caught the light. "Never mind the craftsmanship. Note you the quality of the silver. 'Tis as pure as ever I would dream. See the pale, cool gleam?"

"Yes, sire."

"Your night exploits in the valley yielded enough for this?"

"And, of course, samples from the coal deposit." The

Part II: Honour

servant smiled at his own discovery. "The bauble cost only a pittance for the refining and shaping."

Dryden's lips spread in satisfaction. "Be there enough for a betrothal ring as well?"

The servant's jaw grew slack. "A—a betrothal?" he stammered, a multitude of questions in his eyes.

"Verily. That is what I said." Dryden tapped his free hand impatiently. "Well, is there or not? Answer, man."

He swallowed. "Truly, sire, only half enough."

"Then this shall have to do for the betrothal as well."

The steward nodded, masking his expression. "Yes, sire."

Dryden dismissed the servant with a casual wave of the hand.

Long moments he remained thus at the window, admiring his own wisdom. He turned the band a full circle in the light. A skull, worked into the silver, glimmered. As Dryden rocked it this way and that, the fiendish design danced across his withered cheek.

"My thanks to thee, Sir Robert, for thy demise. This mourning gift 'tis just the beginning of a bountiful harvest from the Mayfield lands. And I shall revel as well in your virgin daughter, the door to uncounted silver, and coal besides!" A low laugh rumbled in Dryden's throat and grew until it filled the entirety of the small room.

* * *

Honour swept into the Great Hall and bent to kiss her mother's cheek.

Catherine, laden with the heavy skirts and headdress of her widow's weeds, was already seated near the massive fireplace.

"Dryden is coming, my dear. He—brings—important matters to discuss."

Honour's brows drew together. "About the estate?"

She looked up at her daughter, then quickly returned her gaze to her lap. Back and forth Catherine twisted the mourning ring, its miniature coffin a constant reminder of their great loss. "Well—yes."

The young lady drew up a marquetry chair beside her mother. Some moments passed in frustrated silence as she arranged her voluminous costume. The extra yardage required for mourning spilled across the arms of the chair onto the floor.

In the muted light from stained glass windows near the beamed ceiling, the mother and daughter formed a startling contrast. Both perfectly attired in respect for Sir Robert, Catherine's old-fashioned black garments only heightened the snowy gown her young daughter wore.

Honour pushed back a strand of dark curls. Her heart beat heavy with foreboding whenever Scudamore was named. She reached for her mother's hand, "Perhaps it is too soon to commit our trust..."

Hoofbeats sounded in the courtyard.

Catherine came alert and drew her hand from Honour's. "Dryden must be improving. He needs not a carriage today."

Honour kept her thoughts to herself. *He shall then plague us more than ever. Better had he shattered ten bones—and one of them his skull.*

* * *

The huge double oak doors swung wide. A servant announced the visitor.

Dryden, attired in his finest suit of clothes, moved across the cold stone, only a slightly irregular gait hinting at his night in the forest. The corners of his mouth twitched as he suppressed the glee threatening to erupt on his features at any moment.

Part II: *Honour*

His irregular eyes noted Catherine at a glance and moved immediately to the vision in white. Honour instinctively slid forward in the chair, as a deer poised to flee the huntsman. When she leaned, the bodice fabric grew taut, revealing her maturing curves.

Dryden touched his tongue to the inside of his lips. *A charming garden of delights, yes,* he thought, as his eyes raked the rest of her.

Catherine's brittle voice drew his attention from his quarry. "Welcome to Mayfield Manor, my neighbour."

"My pleasure, Mistress Mayfield." His tones were entirely too sweet.

The man stretched out a lace-edged cuff to the gentlewoman and kissed her hand. Then bowed deeply to her daughter. "Honour."

With hesitation Honour extended her hand. As his lips lingered on her skin, a string of his greasy hair brushed her wrist. Genteel manners alone forestalled a sudden withdrawal of her greeting.

Sensing her revulsion, Dryden's eyes lowered to the white bodice, reassuring himself with another glimpse of the treasures it promised. With a slow smile, he lifted his gaze to hers and was startled by the challenge there.

Catherine signaled for him to be seated. He drew up another carved chair and lowered himself onto its hand-stitched cushion. In the yawning silence, Dryden very deliberately placed his felt hat on the slates, straightened his jerkin, and adjusted the hose over his injured knee.

Then he leaned forward and cleared his throat. "The time has come when you must make some arrangements for the estate, Mistress Mayfield." His eyes strayed to Honour.

"I, as your near neighbour, am best suited to do so. And willing to sacrifice considerable effort in your behalf."

Catherine nodded, suddenly impatient to get the interview behind her.

"My steward has reviewed your account books, and Mayfield Manor lies on the edge of ruin. Furthermore..."

Honour half rose in her chair. She gripped the armrests. "Who granted permission for your man to inspect our records?"

Dryden leaned toward her, a condescending expression on his face. "Why, your mother, dear one. Is not your own steward bedfast from a hunting accident sustained this week?"

The girl whipped around to face her parent. Honour's countenance was darkened. "Would that you had spoken to me of it first. Have I not adequate cipher and reading skills, learned from my own father?"

The landowner drew in a sharp breath. As Catherine moved to speak, he interceded. "Come, let us address the matters at hand." His voice came smooth, unhurried. "We have not much time to save the manor."

"Save it from what?" Honour pressed. "What conditions lie so dire on this fair place? The fields produce, the cattle multiply, despite the soldiers overrunning the lands." Her voice took on intensity.

Dryden forced a laugh and leaned over to pat her hand. "What does a slip of a girl know of estate management? Why, 'tis nothing suitable for either of you noble ladies to fret your minds." He paused, then plunged on. "Alliance-making is more suitable, is it not, Catherine?"

* * *

Honour turned in confusion to her mother. She read resignation there. "The two of you plan to marry?" the girl ventured.

"Nay, child. Not I." Catherine moved uneasily in her chair, and reached out to touch Honour's face. "It is time for you to wed."

Part II: Honour

The foreboding in Honour's breast exploded. Her lips parted in protest as fear squeezed her soul.

"It is too soon! We yet mourn Father." She clamped her mouth shut, to think, *Yea, the loss of Father brought us to this pass.*

"A little soon, perhaps, dear Honour. But you are ten and seven, and Squire Scudamore has consented to care for you and make good our estate's debts. He even waives the right to a dowry."

Youth's healthy bloom fell from the girl's face, leaving colorless features in its place. "How generous. Nay, you ask too much of me! I shall forever mourn!" Fists clenched until her nails scored the skin. Earlier, unbidden memory of the squire's roaming hands deluged her, and she unconsciously clamped her legs tight together under her skirts.

Catherine held her ground. "When I birthed you in the rooms above this hall, your father chose a curious name to hang upon a bawling infant. When I had rather a conventional one in mind, he insisted on another. 'From the sacred writings,' he said. *'Honour thy father and thy mother...that thy days may be prolonged, and that it may go well with thee...'* She shall be called Honour." Catherine inhaled deeply after the speech, a betrayal of her own haunting doubts.

Honour's face softened slightly at the mention of her father's love for the Book. Her memory stirred at the truth of her mother's words. Vivid was the day she had read those very phrases from the huge manuscript, tracing the command with a chubby finger. Even now, she could almost feel the gentle, firm touch of her father's hand beside hers. She closed her eyes to hold on to him.

Oh, God, for a man like him instead! Not this lying excuse for a gentleman! So vehement was her feeling that she thought for a moment the prayer had escaped her lips.

"I have agreed to the terms," she heard her mother

Circle of Love

saying to Dryden. "Your steward may bring the documents tomorrow morning."

But he was not looking at Catherine. Both of his strange eyes saw only Honour—and all that she would bring to him.

"Then we are betrothed!" Greed's total victory was let loose in the squire's voice. "Shall we seal it with a little kiss?"

As Dryden's hand clamped on the back of her neck, the great doors of the house swung open, startling the trio. A half dozen of His Majesty's soldiers entered, strode noisily across the hall, and made for the grand staircase. Catherine frowned in disapproval.

Honour gladly welcomed the diversion. Her glance strayed across the weary group. She recognized only Richard. And for the first time, she thought, *He does indeed resemble Father!*

* * *

Dryden grunted in disgust at the interruption, bent to pick up his hat, and left Catherine and Honour standing there.

From the doorway, he paused to call out, "I shall return to take Honour riding in the carriage—on the morrow."

As Dryden mounted his horse, the injured knee started hurting again like the devil. But he soon forgot the pain. His sensual fantasies eclipsed all else.

Chapter Fifteen

Captain Allen and the other soldiers mounted the grand staircase. As they reached the second floor, Edward grinned as he leaned toward Richard's ear. "I wonder what sweet little domestic scene we just interrupted? Had I not known better, it appeared the old man was kissing the young mistress."

The captain frowned.

Richard parted from the others and turned toward the wing of the house where his pallet lay. He yawned and dropped onto it, not even removing his boots. Another all-night inspection behind him, he folded the image of the lovely miss to his heart and fell fast asleep.

Near dusk, he awoke to the voices of fellow Cavaliers in the room. "Over at Scudamore's manor...a pair of fine horses...spirited right from under the old man's nose."

Time to review the animals on these lands. Richard rose from the bedding, pulled back on his hat, and went to the stables.

As Richard neared Snowflake's stall, he heard a whinny along with quiet sobbing. Even in its heartbreak, he recognized the cultured voice.

Circle of Love

"Oh, Father—come back! Am—am I chattel to be sold into—vile hands?" She gulped air. "Why have you deserted me?"

Richard seized the truth at once. The soldier raised his hand to the stall door but hesitated. *Dare I to intervene when my presence begets nothing but anger in her?* He ran his hand through his tangled hair. Though his chest tightened, he slipped out into the increasing dusk.

Such a waste for the spirited girl to be turned over to the old wretch, he argued to himself. His boot struck a stone on the footpath, and he gave it a hard kick, then another. *A waste indeed. Especially when my heart grows warm toward her myself, if the truth be told.*

The image of her in Dryden's arms came unbidden, and to his surprise he suddenly struck his fist against a nearby tree. Revulsion rose in his throat. "Would that I could tend her maiden's bloom and purity in his stead!" he whispered, then came to himself and shook his head. "Snowfall in Hades would be more sure."

On the way back to his quarters, Richard wandered the path where Honour had last spoken to him. Several blossoms lay there, bruised and limp. He gazed down, tempted to grind them into dust. Instead, before returning to the house, he slipped one into his jerkin.

* * *

With as little help from Dryden as possible, Honour placed one foot in the carriage. Then she hesitated.

"Perhaps this is not truly proper, having no chaperone," she stalled. "Let us wait until my mother is able to accompany us."

His chiding laugh rumbled low. "Why, of course you are safe. I even bid your grooms accompany us. Are you not yet trusting of your own intended husband?"

Without waiting for a reply, he grasped her firmly at the waist and lifted her the rest of the way into the vehicle. A vein bulged at the side of his neck, and he breathed heavily from the strain, slight as she was.

Then he pulled himself inside, sat down close beside her, and latched the door from the inside. The carriage rumbled across the cobblestones.

Honour moved slightly away from him, spreading out her skirts on the leather seat.

"Shy, my sweet?" he crooned, leaning toward her face. "I bring my betrothed a gift."

He reached into a drawstring bag attached at his waist and drew out a small piece of jewelry.

She bent over to see what the miser offered. A hollow-eyed skull leered at her from the ring of silver. It was badly made, even rough on the edges. And the face produced a crawling sensation up her backbone.

"'Tis a mourning ring, not a betrothal gift." Her voice was sharp.

"Mistress Mayfield sports a similar piece, and I know how attached you are to your departed father—and to the, ah, season of mourning!"

Then he cackled and slapped his good leg. "Verily, I owe him a debt for dying and leaving you for me. It makes not a bad prenuptial gift at all, I think."

She straightened and set her lips. "In view of your—gracious gift, I should then wear deep mourning for the wedding."

"It matters not to me what you put on your body that day. I shall remove it from you soon enough."

Honour shivered. And instead of placing the gift on her hand properly, she held it lightly between her fingertips. As if she wished to limit the ring's contact with her skin.

They jostled in silence until he grew conversational again. "Allow me to tell you of your new home. As mistress of the manor, you will want to know many things."

He droned on and on, as the carriage wound its way through the countryside. Eventually it left the Mayfield lands, traveling southward just along the edge of Dryden's property.

A deep rut jolted the carriage and threw Honour against the graying squire. He snatched at the opportunity, and grasped her firmly against his side. Her many layered garments insulated her from his touch, but inwardly she recoiled.

"Ah, there is no need to be coy with me. Not many days from now, we shall share the marriage bed." His lips twisted into a wicked smile, as his hand roamed for soft flesh.

"That day is not yet." Her response was firm.

"But I should like a small taste of my virgin bride, to be certain that she is sweet and not bitter."

A cry of alarm went off in Honour's mind. "Nay!" She moved his hand away from her hip. "A bride must approach marriage undefiled."

"Narry but a few come untried, I warrant. Else, how would a gentleman gain his experience!" He drew his other arm tighter around her. "A little trifle before—no harm."

Honour's voice grew frigid as her fear mounted. "Nay. Nay, I say!"

Dryden suddenly placed his thigh well across her skirt, pinning her to the seat. "I...said...I shall have a little taste."

He snatched off her head covering and threw it to the floor, freeing her rich curls to the feel of his hands. She tossed her head to and fro to dislodge his grip, but he locked onto the sides of her face and drew his head toward hers. Thin lips, oozing saliva, covered hers, punishing and bruising all they took possession of.

"You owed me that, girl," he muttered against her nose. "Those bloody soldiers ruined my betrothal kiss, but I shall have all I want now."

Part II: Honour

Soon discontent with so small a revelation, he groped at her bodice. Finding but fistfuls of yard goods, he charged at the intricate fastenings of her gown with both hands. "No longer the girl-child that sat upon my lap, but a woman."

She backed into the corner of the carriage and drew up a knee against him. Still he came upon her.

As she leaned down to escape him and fetch her head-covering, she lost her balance and slid to the floor of the carriage. The ring clinked on the wood beside her. He followed her down, trying to shove his arm up her white skirts. His nails scraped and dug at her flesh.

But he stopped midway, bellowing in pain. His knee had come to rest atop the ring. Gingerly, he moved his leg and clasped the jewelry. Honour caught a breath, then sank her teeth into his forearm.

Naked hatred creased his face. With his free hand, he grasped the neck of her gown and gave a mighty pull. The fabric cut off her air passage briefly, then gave way. She resisted, and the dress ripped to the waist, exposing her. Like a dog gone mad, Dryden dropped his mouth onto her breast and bit with all his might.

Her cry of pain nearly knocked the driver off his perch. But by the time he had brought the carriage to a safe halt, Dryden had abused her body more. Her tender skin bore not only teeth marks but hideous bruises, each one in the shape of a skull.

As Jack forced open the carriage door, Honour barely glimpsed her saviours' faces. For Dryden struck her head on the floorboards, and she lost consciousness.

* * *

That night, Honour lay awake behind the bed curtains, stiff and staring with dry eyes, mindless of the rich brocaded patterns. The last candle burned itself out. Then in the blanketing dark, she clutched a linen-encased pillow and buried her face in it. Finally, her narrow shoulders bent, and the bitter tears came. Clammy hands shook as they tentatively traced the bruises from the day's events.

If that truly is marriage, I need no part in it. She shuddered.

Ghastly multi-faced visions of Dryden leered at her from all sides. Fingers splayed, Honour's hands pushed fruitlessly against the blackness. Her braided hair worked loose as she tossed on the pillow. For hours, she lay trapped by fear, like a tiny gray dove. Finally, with a shudder of exhaustion, she drifted into a dream-tossed, uneasy sleep.

* * *

The night watcher's mount suddenly reared and whinnied. Richard muttered sharply at Snowflake, "What the devil?" and looked toward the manor, its turrets and chimneys just visible in the pale moonlight. *Was there a sound?* Removing his hat, he listened intently. Rocks grated and shifted. A vague splash at the lake reached his ears.

His alert eyes searched the sheening surface, rewarded by a flash of something white, just below the old stone bridge. Then whatever it was disappeared, suddenly as it had come.

Instinctively, Snowflake headed for the place, before Richard could even give the command. Her mane streaked back, hooves covered the short distance rapidly, and Richard felt an eerie foreboding in his stomach.

The nimble horse halted too quickly at the edge, nearly tossing Richard overhead into the dark water, next to the crumbled stonework. Grotesque tree fingers, bony bare of leaves, clawed at his long, curling hair as if to slow his unsteady dismount. He set his candle lantern abruptly on the ground.

Momentarily, a wide fan of black silken threads surfaced on the water. *God help me, 'tis Honour!* A hammering heart joined the sickness in his soul. He stripped off his leather buff-coat in one fluid motion, flinging it beneath an ancient fir, and half-waded, half-dived into the murky ink. Straining toward the great emptiness that had held the beautiful fan, Richard felt the chill water snatch at his lungs. He grimaced, drew a deep breath, and dove further into the dark water. His hands swept through the deep, but came up agonizingly empty.

Another dive. His strong hands searched below the surface and came in contact with cloth, then felt it slip away. He tried again, and grasped his treasure in tight fingers. As he swam back toward the shore, the fabric gave way, and frantically he grabbed at the cloth and gripped flesh.

Nearly blinded by the lengths of hair that swam around his eyes, Richard reached the muddy lake edge. Stumbling up the mossy bank, cradling the limp figure in his arms, he paused to look into Honour's dear, still face. Dripping, he knelt down and gently placed the girl in the shelter of the evergreen, on a soft nature-made pallet.

The wringing nightdress clung to Honour's maidenly curves, and its torn places revealed beauty he'd only dared imagine. Lightly, he laid a droplet-covered hand near her heart. At his touch, she stirred ever so slightly. Richard's blood shot through his veins like lightning, fueled by elation—and desire.

In a quick frenzy, he ran his hands from the hollow of her throat, down and across her body—stroking, massaging, urging her to life. Still kneeling over her, Richard looked heavenward through the branches of the age-old tree. "Oh, Father God, give her breath—and make her mine!" The intense voice reverberated in the verdant room.

The girl stirred, then her eyes flickered briefly.

"Honour, my little dove," he rasped, snatching her by

the shoulders and lifting her toward his chest. "Live! Breathe! I love you!"

Mindful for the first time of gooseflesh against him, Richard cradled her with one arm, while he reached for his coat with the other, silently chiding himself for his selfish desire. The only dry clothing available soon enveloped Honour's chilled body, and she nestled against him. The warmth, the recollection of his new yet familiar touch, teased her whole being toward awareness.

A pine cone dropped from above onto Richard's shoulder. As he flinched, she groaned slightly. Then a sputter came from her throat. Instinctively, he turned her body to the side and held her head.

After a long siege of coughing, Honour's eyes widened. Richard rejoiced in her response. He took in her astonishment as she struggled to place the owner of the strong arms, light hair, and gently-timbred voice.

"Why, Richard Allen!" She turned her head around in confusion. "You could not be the one who is chasing—bruising..." She trailed off, choked again, and reached a tentative hand toward her still sore lips. Her glance dropped from Richard's expressive eyes to his clothing, wet as hers. "You. You must be my friend. Not Dryden!" Her thin shoulders shuddered at the name.

Richard drew the buff-coat tighter around her, feeling with relief some warmth from her own body. "No, I'm not Dryden. I am only the one who has loved you since the day in the library. The one who's desperately miserable at the loss of you—whether to the murky lake or that black-hearted scoundrel of a Scudamore."

He bit his lip at the declaration, fairly tasting his ordinariness as a second son, with so little to offer. And not only that, but a soldier billeted in her family home—a daily thorn, a reminder of England at enmity with itself and of her father's fate.

Part II: Honour

Snowflake whinnied. Richard grimaced at this recollection, too, of Honour's earlier fury at him. *Even tonight, I ride her prized possession.*

'Tis no use, anyway. The thought pierced his heart. His gaze rested again on the innocent one he loved, about to be given to her beastly neighbour. The soldier straightened abruptly, almost upsetting her precarious balance as well. *It cannot be!*

"Honour. Why are you so frightened of that man? What has he done?" His voice was gentle, coaxing.

She grasped him as in a vise and clung, nails digging into Richard's broad back. "He—he—afternoon last in the carriage...He grabbed me—t-tore my dress." Her voice broke into a gulping sob. It was awhile before she could continue. "I'm so afraid! I was trying to get away. I—I couldn't stand to have him touching me..." She raised fingertips to her lips. "Oh, how he hurt me."

Richard turned her face toward his in the near-dark. He spoke very softly. "So you tried to get away?"

"Oh, verily, I did! But I was trapped in the carriage. He tried to do unspeakable things."

"Before the servants?"

"Yes, Roger and Jack drove the coach," she choked. "Dryden tore the laces and bit me..." She shook as she placed a hand on the coat covering her injured breast. "H—here."

Richard swore. Bile rose to the back of his throat, even as he continued to comfort her in his arms. "Is that what brought you from the house this night? Did he haunt your dreams as well?"

She gulped. "Yes. I was r—running. His face was all around. His teeth..."

"So you ran out into the night and slipped off the old bridge into the water?" His hand brushed against her wet gown.

"Did I? Truly, I cannot remember." She sagged, out of breath. Richard kept silence, as well, using the opportunity to brace his weary back against the shaggy tree trunk.

"If God cares for the helpless, there must be some way to prevent marriage to this awful beast," he ventured tentatively.

"I know of none." She shook her head helplessly. "Mother fears him—and Father is—gone. The plans are sealed."

She burrowed her wet mane against his neck. "Drowning would have been better..." She shuddered. "I'm so sorry—so ungrateful."

Though the soldier could barely hear her muffled voice, he felt a strange pricking against his eyelids.

Gently, Richard's arms fitted her to him. Time meant nothing as he cradled and stroked, bringing her comfort. Gradually, her storm gave way to calm. Almost on its own, Honour's clasp on him grew firmer, causing his heart to flare with hope.

"Dear, precious Honour. If I could find some way to free you from this union with him..." He ran his fingers through her tangled tresses to gather courage. "...dare I think you might have me?" His breath stood still, awaiting her answer.

A breeze whispered through the scented curtains of the protector tree. Only a few strides away, Snowflake pawed the damp earth with a hoof.

"Heaven help me. I—I believe I could love you, indeed, Richard Allen." And, like a sunray that dances for just an instant, then is gone, she brushed her bruised lips below his ear.

With that one kiss, she unleashed a dam of feeling in the man. He ached for her—body and soul—and could not resist pulling her close again, this time with Honour's full awareness of his actions. So different were they from Dryden's. Near desperation welled up in him, fighting

Part II: Honour

against control.

"There must be a way. If God is in His heaven, there is—somewhere." His mustache tickled the sweet hollow of her throat, and she shivered again.

"Still cold?"

"No. I fear my yearnings betray my duty." Despite her pain, she glowed from the womanliness he had awakened.

Richard sighed with joy. "Marriage betwixt us would yield a pleasant duty, my little dove."

"You have a gentle touch. For all your strength, no fear do you inspire."

"You sense rightly. I would cherish and protect you. But that is only if I can find a way for us."

Honour bowed her head. "Please, God, do."

"Keep strict silence, Honour. But meet me two days hence—at the abandoned iron forge. I pray by then I shall know what to do." He paused. "You can reach the place without suspicion?"

"Oh, yes, Richard," she laughed suddenly, lightly. "Remember, I used to go all over the manor—before you took such a liking to Snowflake?" He heard the forgiveness in her words.

"And before soldiers swarmed across the land, only too glad to plague an innocent beauty," he rejoined.

A cloud passed across his brow. "Honour, do you realize a way out may mean leaving Mayfield Manor—and even perhaps England—forever?"

Her head drooped and damp strands curtained her face. "Yes, I know that full well." She looked up at him, love in her eyes. "…and I am willing."

Richard lifted Honour and bore her through the shadows. Then set her on her feet. "I dare not be seen with you. Do your limbs support you?"

She gingerly set one foot before the other. "Yes."

"Away, then, to your dry bed, and sleep much of the

morrow. You may need all your strength. When the bells strike four, two days hence, you'll find me at the forge." He gently clasped her body to his and placed his lips on her sodden hair. The feel of her took his breath away.

"Richard. Make a way, please!"

He brushed aside a low fir branch. There across the lake lay the sleeping manor. Just as Honour gathered the gown's bodice in her fist, Richard glimpsed a creamy swell in the moonlight.

Ah, indeed I must. He smiled as he watched her steal across the hill. Richard mounted Snowflake, turning the mare toward the stables and a change of clothes. As he waited, watching over his shoulder, an idea began to form and take root. Through the moonlit night, he could just distinguish the girl's lithe figure, as she drew nigh the safest door. There was an unexpected lightness to her step that made his heart sing.

Chapter Sixteen

*H*onour awakened unusually early, after spending all the previous day in the narrow bed. As she pulled back the brocade to set her feet on the floor, foreboding and excitement fluttered together in her breast. She walked over to the casement to behold thousands of acres bathed in dawn's pink light. Mayfield land. Home. Birds warbled their morning songs.

In the pit of Honour's stomach, the battle continued. *Oh, to be carefree as that sparrow, unencumbered as a lily of the field!* she mused. The knowledge she carried of this day's meeting—and what it could mean—both burdened and thrilled her. *Richard, my love, are you horsed and already at your guard post?* she wondered.

The day ahead already seemed an eternity, until the time she could slip out of the household to the rendezvous at the old iron forge.

First, Molly brought breakfast, then she insisted on a longer than usual soak in the bath. "With the wedding nigh, you must take time for the fragrant oils." The servant winked.

Honour voiced no argument. *Not one drop for Dryden, but all for Richard*, she thought, as she stepped into the fragrant water. Honour cleansed the lake silt from her hair. Then she closed her eyes, wondering what help the meeting would bring.

* * *

All day in the cavernous house, time dragged more slowly than a sundial on a cloudy day. At the third-hour bell in the afternoon, Honour returned to her room to view her face in the looking glass. She straightened a curl, and pinched her pale cheeks. It was time to depart for the forge.

She exited through the Great Hall, with its plain beamed ceiling and fireplace so massive a servant could stand full-height in it. Her glance fell on the imposing coat of arms over the fireplace and traveled to the small shields along the stone walls. All told of marriages in the Mayfield line. *And what of my union? What arms—if any—will link with these?* She almost spoke aloud.

Startled by her own thoughts, Honour glanced around. No one was about for the moment. Pulling on her mantle, sure to be needed against the coming shade, she passed through the hall's last arch and out the double oak doors. To satisfy any onlookers, especially anyone at the oriel window over the door, she walked straight away from the house, down the lane toward the village.

But at the first crossroad, Honour swung hard right, passing through the secluded ivy-covered walkway that protected her from all view of the house and led toward the abandoned forge.

She arrived at the isolated shanty soon after the fourth bell had rung.

A familiar whinny in the wood assured her Snowflake was nearby. Honour parted the vines camouflaging the forge's entryway, and there indeed stood Richard, waiting. His clothing was rumpled, and his feathered hat sat at a

Part II: Honour

rakish angle on his handsome head. There were lines of fatigue and worry around his eyes.

The man stretched out both arms immediately and folded her to him. "My love, you came." His voice was husky. "We must not meet long today. It is surely dangerous."

She accepted his kiss and returned it with a fluttery one of her own, secretly wanting more. "I had to come. I know I love you." Her chin trembled slightly. "But I am so afraid."

"I have developed a plan. It is perilous, but—your life with Dryden would be more perilous still."

He reached into the breast of his uniform and drew out a small missive. "Herein lies my father's last letter. I fetched it from safekeeping a day's ride from this place."

Richard saw her puzzled look, as he leaned toward the doorway's light. "'Tis very brief. Let me read it to you."

As he repeated the sparse message, Honour's expression lifted with hope. "Might he...?"

"He might. I must ride hard for London and pray for a way to see the Lord Bishop."

"Does he remain in the Tower, as my father said months ago?"

"I shall be very careful—and seek to communicate with him."

"Perchance you cannot return in time. Then what?"

Richard's face clouded a moment, then his brows formed a hard line. "I dare not think of that! Besides, do you not believe the Almighty can be trusted to care for us? Has He not preserved our lives in England's struggle—and revealed to us our own?"

He continued, with greater intensity. "Remember the words the old priest read only days ago from St. Matthew six—

> *"Therefore I say unto you, 'Take no thought for your life....Behold the fowls of the air: for*

they sow not, neither do they reap, nor gather into barns, yet your heavenly father feedeth them. Are ye not much better than they?'"

"Yes, dear Richard, I do remember. He recited, as well, not to be anxious about tomorrow. But before he closed the book, the lesson gave a warning, '...*sufficient unto the day is the evil thereof.*'"

"True. In trying to spare you desperate misery with Dryden, I threaten a new sorrow." He reached for her slim hand in the fading light. "Your promise to me—in the face of family and duty—means more than life itself. I pledge to guard you with my last breath, if need be, so help me God."

Snowflake pawed and neighed. The sound of a cart's creaking along a nearby track reached them in the hiding place.

Richard's deep-timbred voice dropped to a whisper. "Thou, Lord, made blind eyes to see. Now I beg thee to make enemy eyes blind, both now and until that night. Amen."

He clasped Honour to him once more with intensity, kissed her silent lips, and pressed her toward the outside air.

She turned back toward him from the opening. "You will get a message to me?"

"Through my faithful lieutenant Edward. Trust only him—and God."

"Godspeed," she whispered, as her soft footfalls led her away into the woods.

* * *

Richard approached London with more than ordinary caution. News gleaned in furtive conversations along the way prepared him for a city steeped in turmoil.

Around the perimeter of the city arose a patchy system of defense. Peasant folk, even women and children, dug ditches and carried materials for the emerging forts not yet joined together.

He shuddered at a populace so stirred up as to build defenses against its own ruler.

As the lone rider skirted the properties of Whitehall, he glimpsed tall grass growing in the empty courtyard of the King's palace. *An affront not only to His Majesty but even to Inigo Jones' creative design as well*, he thought.

Snowflake shied as they crossed the bridge over the Thames. Richard reined in tightly and reassured her with a light stroke along the neck. The smell of rotting flesh—from human heads displayed on the bridge—mingled with the general stench of the river. And as he watched workers unload a ship at the quay, Richard wondered if King Charles would still control the navy, had he not demanded so much ship money in his desperation for taxes.

Between Vauxhall and Halfway Forts, Richard stabled the horse and strode purposely across the cobblestones toward Lambeth Palace. Despite the changing political winds, the everyday sounds of London mingled all around him. A farmer whipped his carthorse. A stray dog darted after a black rat. A dirty ragamuffin bumped against the soldier's leg, causing him to catch his tall boots against one another and break stride. Richard gripped his purse tighter and set his eyes on the red brick building.

The imposing structure commanded the south side of the Thames and stood out regally from the poorer lath, plaster, and pitch buildings common to the area. As he approached the gateway to the palace, Richard reached for his plumed hat and tucked it under his arm. His hair, given more care that morning, shined bright in the sun for an instant. Then he found himself in the shade of the twin towers of five storeys each. He brushed the front of his clothing, from sash to knees, and dust powdered the walkway.

A gatekeeper with cropped hair looked him up and down. "State your name and business."

"Richard Allen. I have a letter concerning the Archbishop."

Something between a cackle and a sneer came out of the keeper's mouth. "Then maybe ye belong at the Tower rather than here—that is, if you can get in—or out."

Richard struggled to remain above the low-class insolence of the fellow. But he raised his voice, and emotion betrayed the York accent. "'Tis a matter of great urgency. Perhaps one of the lesser bishops..." He peered beyond the barrier and saw a robed man sitting in the outer court with a book. "...or a secretary remains at the palace."

As the guard planted his legs and stretched his arms to bar entry, he called out, "Try again tomorrow. Mayhap the Puritans will change their minds and let the miserable persecutor free."

He laughed in derision. "Or I'll decide to humor ye, after all."

Richard's soul cried out within, *Dear God, I must get through today. Tomorrow will be too late!*

Just then, a balding man inside turned his head and stood abruptly. He squinted and shaded his eyes with a hand. It took little time for him to cover the distance to the gate. His dark eyes flashed a warning as he motioned the guard to step aside.

An authoritative voice boomed. "Do I see rightly? Can it be Richard Allen?"

"Yes!" Richard grasped his outstretched hand. "John Rutledge! God be praised!"

Rutledge turned to the sour-faced gateman. "Admit him. I take full responsibility for his presence. Harass him not. Do you understand?"

Part II: Honour

The man turned back to others at the gate with no further word.

Richard fell in step beside his former tutor.

"Let me show you the splendid ceilings of the guard room." His voice was overloud. Rutledge rounded a ivy-covered wall, which led to the Bishops Walk along the Thames. There, he grasped Richard's sleeve and murmured quietly, "Come with me to the great quadrangle. There we can converse without being overheard."

"I am much relieved for your intervention. And delighted for the sight of you again."

"What a man you have become."

Through a succession of arched corridors, the cleric led his former pupil. Finally, they emerged out of doors again, away from the large ears of the churchman's enemies.

"Why have you risked coming here, and what do you need?"

"I—I..." Speech faltered while he reached into his buttoned breast for a paper. "My father—This is the last missive I received before he died. In it, he said thus:

> *My second son,*
> *The tide of battle may yet sweep me away from this earth. Need you a severe strong arm in time of trouble, be not afraid to approach Lord Bishop William Laud. Though criticism of his methods and power abound, I have his pledge of influence for all my sons.*

Richard handed Rutledge the letter. "I am in deep need of the Archbishop's help. But I also fear to presume for it, even if a message can be got to him."

The keen eyes softened. "You have come here rightly. For Laud owes your father a great debt, in fact, his life itself."

Circle of Love

Richard leaned forward. "'Tisn't much of a life now, if indeed he remains in the Tower, as I've heard."

"But I assure you he remembers, for he told me of it. Only weeks before your father's life candle was snuffed, he was assigned to travel with the Archbishop. Your father's shout gave early warning of attack. His keen escort, and placement of himself before the cutthroats, gave back a life very nearly taken."

"I never knew of that." Richard stroked his pointed beard thoughtfully. "Father was loyal, above else."

"Indeed." Richard's teacher paced back and forth over the stones. "Now, you are in serious trouble of some kind."

"But Laud is in a graver situation."

"Yes, and no. Indeed, Parliament has impeached him and then sent him to the Tower." He controlled his big voice carefully. "He is likely to be charged with high treason. But for those loyal to the Crown, he remains Archbishop of Canterbury, the highest churchman in all England. The King has not renounced him. And the Royalists may well prevail over Parliament."

"Yet, I have no access to him to plead for me. My need is desperate and immediate."

Rutledge smiled. "I am permitted to see him often. Parliament brought me here for the purpose of gathering the diaries of William Laud, making copies, and editing them to assure his guilt." He put his mouth near Richard's ear. "It's a dangerous but useful game I'm playing. I appear to cooperate for now but at the first opportunity will destroy all I can and flee to York. There I shall assist the King in printing his Majesty's pamphlets. Even now a press lies waiting near York Minster Cathedral."

Speech failed Richard for a moment, as he pondered the daring of his tutor's game. "When do you visit the Tower next?"

"This evening."

Part II: Honour

Earnest hope broke onto Richard's visage. He leaned closer. "It is a bold and personal request, sir. It concerns Honour Mayfield, daughter of Sir Robert Mayfield of Keele. He died at Edgehill in the King's Lifeguards. I ask a revoked license and nullified settlement for her marriage four days hence to Dryden Scudamore, and for a Special License to marry her myself." He exhaled suddenly and looked at his hands.

"I presume you realize the import of your request. There must be some extraordinary circumstances involved?"

"Yes! Scudamore aspires to engulf the entire Mayfield Manor through his marriage to Honour..."

"That in itself is hardly unusual."

"Scudamore viciously attacked her only days ago. I bear a letter in her own writing, signed by two eyewitnesses testifying to his savagery."

The churchman accepted the parchment. "The writing of a girl, witnessed by servants using a mark for a name." A frown creased his learned brow. "Yet I do recall a very nasty event of murder and sacrilege at Barthomley."

"Scudamore's work. The man is a sadistic infidel."

"So I am to request the negation of the local license on the basis of cruelty, allowing you to marry her, thus thwarting his plans on both accounts?"

"Exactly." Richard's chest filled and he straightened. "Besides, I have come to love her deeply myself and wish to rescue her from his talons."

The teacher nodded knowingly. "So you admit you do have mingled motives." His keen eyes missed nothing.

"Yea, my desire to protect and care for her is tinged with another, ah, more carnal one. I am nigh to committing sin with her—in my heart."

"My student, you have remembered your holy studies well. Indeed, Jesus declared that to look on a woman with lust was sin, not just the lying with her. But our Maker also willed that man and woman become one flesh, and He established the sacrament of marriage at the beginning of time."

"Unmarried as I am, her maidenhood belongs to me—in my dreams. In some moments, I ponder what sets me apart from the evil Dryden who in the flesh near tore it from her? His is a dastardly evil, mine only more subtle, though mingled with noble cause. Rutledge, this once-priest now finds himself in need of one."

The older man placed his hand on the head of the younger. "Come with me. Let us go into the chapel to pray."

After very private moments, man with man and man with God, Richard and his tutor arose from their knees. They folded down seats from the richly carved paneling and sat beside one another.

"Tell me. What does Honour say? Has she expressed her heart?"

"She is with me in this. We have spoken together."

"But will not dishonour fall immediately upon your heads, after the deed is discovered?"

Richard ran a hand through the long forelocks of his hair. "Indeed, it is expected. I plan a new start for us—in the New World. There is money to purchase passage. As a second son, I have little to hold me here."

"What of the girl's widowed mother?"

"She has a son fighting on the Continent. A missive this week indicates Andrew, though wounded, is attempting to return home shortly. We shall endeavor to send word to Lady Catherine, once we are safely away."

"I will take your request to the Archbishop tonight." He stood. "Come to my room. We must draw up documents." The churchman turned to Richard, placing a heavy hand on his shoulder. "I shall explain every detail of what must be done. Hear me carefully."

After a painstaking time of preparation, the papers were

Part II: Honour

completed. Rutledge ordered venison and bread for Richard, offered his bed to the traveler for a few hours rest, and departed for the Tower.

* * *

John Rutledge returned late, with a look of satisfaction on his face. The cleric's final admonition etched itself deeply in Richard's mind. "Guard the documents with your life, if you wish your bride and offspring to have any honour at all. And—we shall not likely see one another again in this life. The Lord watch over you, my young friend."

At midnight, Richard left Lambeth without having to face the gatekeeper again. A hot meal and excellent wine warming his insides, he mounted Snowflake and rode through the city streets toward the Oxford road.

Even at the late hour, he had to dodge a slop pot's spray in one narrow passage. A few drops on his hat, no matter, but the documents secured between his thumping chest and saddle-weary loins must remain dry.

I must ride as far as possible under cover of darkness, he thought. A full moon smiled upon him, illuminating the road cut between fields and meadows. He kept watch for ravines and trees to hide himself, should he hear another traveler approach.

And his pulse quickened as he remembered Honour's face, and the innocent warmth of her, waiting for him. *Every gallop brings me closer. Press on, Snowflake, to your mistress. Take me to her—in time!*

* * *

When her thread tangled the fifth time, Honour laid down her tapestry work. She found it hard to stay her fingers, and her mind. After she donned suitable attire for outdoors, she slipped out the library portal toward the stables.

Snowflake's place was indeed empty.

Jack came out of a nearby stall. "Looking for Snowflake, milady?"

"I—I merely wanted to see for myself how she fares. I ride her not at all since His Majesty's soldiers came."

"She's been gone almost two days, and him that's been keeping watch on her, too." The wrinkled groom shook his head. "'Tis a puzzle, him leaving with that band of Roundheads encamped only two miles away."

Honour looked down at the straw, lest she reveal to the faithful servant her knowledge of Richard's errand. And her surprise at Parliament's forces this far north.

On the ivy-covered pathway back to the house, Honour clasped her hands at her stomach so tightly they hurt. She wondered how Richard fared at Lambeth Palace, and whether he would return in time. Then she prayed.

* * *

Richard rode throughout the night. Shortly after dawn, he drew up the horse at an obscure village and slipped inside the nearest tavern.

"Have you a bed for a few hours?"

The toothless crone smiled broadly. "One shilling. Be ye needing anything else—a wench to warm it, mayhap?" She paused. "Only double the price." Her eyes glinted, as she pointed to a slip of a girl serving tankards of ale. "Have her all ye want, with never a ring in yer nose." She threw back her head and cackled.

"Only the bed. Be certain of that." Richard drew coin from his purse. "I shall tend the horse myself."

Emerging from the low door back out onto the lane, the soldier glanced dully ahead. From a half-timbered house

Part II: Honour

dangled a silversmith's guild sign.

One of the old woman's words echoed in his weary soul. *Ring. Why, I have no ring for my bride!*

With new purpose to his step, the traveler reached the hitching post, then led Snowflake into a tavern stall. The man sniffed the brackish water and fingered moldy hay. He turned to see a young lad shuffle forward.

"I kin care for your big animal."

"See that my mount has *clean* water and *fresh* hay." Richard emphasized his demands with a few pence dropped into a grubby palm.

The boy's eyes brightened. "I want to grow up brave and tall like you, and fight in His Majesty's guards."

Richard stood still. "I pray when you reach manhood we yet have a king." He spoke softly, shoulders slumped, not certain the child even heard. Abruptly, he straightened and turned out into the morning sun.

Now for a place to lay my bones awhile. And then, a ring.

* * *

After a restless sleep, Richard emerged from the inn, and his eyes flicked the tradesman's sign. *Nothing but cheap trinkets to be found in a place like this,* he reasoned, yet he crossed the rutted lane in but a few strides.

The hearth illuminated an interior unlike the shabby tavern. His eyes moved from the sparse, purposeful furnishings to the neatly ordered tools and, on a piece of soft cloth, several brooches. No slackness here.

A wizened smith looked up from a small book to greet his visitor. Shocks of argent hair nearly matched the metal in which he worked. Direct eyes and lines of laughter marked the ruddy face.

"Wh—what bringeth such a st—stranger to m—me this

Circle of Love

d—day? A b—bauble for the soldier's l—lady?"

Richard's eyebrows registered his surprise at the man's speech. He picked up a brooch. The work was good. "Well, I, ah...A ring for a lady. Yes. A beloved lady." He breathed out in a rush. "Have you anything suitable?"

The craftsman turned on his stool. "A w—wee trifle to entertain the l—lady." He pushed back his hair, all the while studying Richard. "Or mayhap it m—means more—an object of lasting beau—beauty. This?"

He passed over the brooches and reached a skilled hand toward a piece of jewelry still on the bench.

A perfect band of silver gleamed in the yellow light. The craftsman offered it to Richard.

"My—my own design. None other like it, in all the k—kingdom."

Dainty rosebuds, with spirals of ivy, embraced a pronouncement of love. The soldier turned the circlet slowly in his outstretched hand. "Thou and thou only," he murmured, a bittersweet catch in his throat.

Wise words came from the older man. "A cir—circle of l—love. W—without end."

Richard's hand engulfed the ring, as he shot a fervent prayer upward, to keep company the many already thus sent. *Only by God's doing*, he thought.

It is right. Right for my innocent beauty. He pulled out the leather purse. "I can offer no more than this." He held up a single gold coin which bore the image of an angel. "His Majesty lags behind on my pay."

The guildman smiled. "D—done."

"I should like it engraved—thus." Richard reached for a scrap of leather and marked it.

The silversmith motioned for Richard to sit down. The soldier sank straightaway into a corner of the shop. To the rhythmical sounds of etching, he nodded off.

When a tankard clattered against a trencher, Richard

Part II: Honour

opened his eyes and sat up.

"The r—ring is finished. You need both r-rest and sustenance, my way—wayfarer friend."

"Indeed, I am beholden to you."

Richard licked his lips at the bread and cheese his host offered. He reached for a loaf, then drew in his hand quickly. The craftsman looked up toward the rafters, giving thanks in his halting way.

After the simple repast, the elder of the two crossed to his bench and showed forth his handiwork.

"R.A. et H.M. But what is this additional?" Richard's face registered disappointment.

"Ah. I have taken the l—liberty of adding my maker's mark to this r—ring of l—love, and a reference from the Holy Wr—Writ."

"Go on."

"First Epistle of S—St. John, fourth chapter, v—verse 19. *'We love him: because he first loved us.'*" He pointed to the rare book beside him. "The only r...real source of love."

"Indeed. I am obliged to you."

With that, the man enclosed the ring in a velvet drawstring bag and entrusted it to the soldier. As Richard paused under the lintel to wave, the man looked steadily at him. "Godspeed."

Chapter Seventeen

The days since Richard's departure had passed indeed slowly. Honour spent long hours in the library, bent over the precious manuscript she and her father once shared together. She read over and over the fifth and sixth chapters of Ephesians.

One entire afternoon, she sat making entries in her journal before the oriel window. Its irregular glass seemed to cloud over with tears—but in truth, the mist came from Honour's eyes. Honour. *Honour thy father and thy mother*—the command pierced deep. Likewise another. *Husbands, love your wives, even as Christ also loved the Church, and gave himself for it.* Caught between them, she fell to her knees.

That evening, she strolled the courtyard, never going beyond the manor's walled security. Her eyes cast down, Honour paid no attention to the sentry at the gate. Until he whispered her name. Straining her eyes in the gathering dusk, she discerned his face. The soldier she had seen so often at Richard's side.

"Edward." Her lips barely moved.

"Honour, milady." He inclined his head downward, as if

no further discourse passed betwixt them. "Be at the dairy barn, the night before the planned nuptials, as the eleventh hour approaches."

She pressed her hand to her pounding heart, and measured her steps carefully back to the house. *Will he come in time?*

* * *

Two afternoons later, Honour and her mother stood before the oak wardrobe. Within it hung the wedding dress. Across the room, Molly rearranged the pots of creams and oils before the looking glass, then the maid stepped around the curtained bed and joined the bride and her mother.

As Catherine opened the ornately carved doors, rich folds of the purple gown cascaded to the floor. The low square-necked bodice and slashed sleeves gave off a silken sheen, softened by a layering of intricate lace. Strands of tiny pearls formed loops so delicate they merely kissed the gauze-like inset here and there. From the delicate cap flowed abundant lace, lovingly made in a cottage on the estate. Its silken ribbons floated toward the women like a mist.

As the bride's mother reached to fluff the folds, a shadow passed across Honour's pale face. She stared at the exquisite bodice until the pearls swam together.

The maid bent toward Honour. "Is there anything amiss?" Molly's concern etched new lines in her face. Catherine, too, looked up from the dress to search her daughter's eyes.

Honour stared down at the floor and shook her dark head hesitantly. She couldn't trust her voice. It sought to betray her.

Catherine reached for her hand and patted it softly. "It's normal to be nervous, my dear, on the eve of marriage. Your life will change, indeed, but you won't be far away..."

Honour's throat constricted. A hollow feeling pierced her heart.

The lady of the manor walked over to the casement and drew back the heavy brocade. Through the trees stood the spire of the stone church. "Tomorrow will be a beautiful day. I only wish—wish your father were still here with us," Catherine murmured. Her hand on the drapes trembled.

Honour thought, *Were Father here, there would be no need of a wedding.*

Turning to face the girl and her servant, Catherine regained her composure and forced brightness to her voice. "How joyously those bells will sound tomorrow!" She suddenly put her fingertip on her temple. "Goodness! I neglected to tell you Dryden stopped in while you were out walking. He and the young curate seem to have it all planned and in order. And they put aside the convention of mourning, due to our circumstances. Your father would understand."

She directed her attention to the servant. "Molly, be sure to remember the flowers to trim the headpiece. They're to be cut very early in the morning."

"Yes, milady. I'll see to it; you can be certain."

"Thank you, Molly. You may leave my daughter and me alone for awhile."

The door closed softly. Catherine put her arm around Honour's shoulders. "I have something very special for your wedding day."

Reaching into the drawstring purse suspended from her gown, the handsome woman brought out a miniature chest. "You know of the long tradition in my family, the heirloom passed from each eldest daughter to the next generation."

Honour nodded and smiled. "Indeed, I do. You showed it to me once when I was much younger."

"That I did. And now it is to be yours. Do you also recall the medallion's story? How it was fashioned in 1356 from booty seized at the Battle of Poitier? It bears an ancient crest. The *fleur de lis* was proudly added to our arms to proclaim the victory, thus the *fleur de lis* with the scythe."

Catherine lovingly opened the chest and turned the small treasure toward her daughter. Even in the fading daylight, the image flashed its golden radiance. In the center stood the embossed design, caressed by the years.

Honour gasped. "Oh, mother, 'tis far more beautiful than I remember." Her hand rose, trembling, and she received the open jewel box into her fingers. Tears she'd been fighting all afternoon finally had their way.

The older woman wisely kept silence, comforting her with a loving embrace.

Muffled by Catherine's shoulder, Honour gulped, "I shall treasure your generosity always." Then she straightened and clenched her left fist. *Though I am unworthy to wear it.*

Honour took a step back and her eyes met her mother's. "No matter what," she spoke with a strange tremor in her voice, "I beg your trust in me."

"Why, of course, Honour. Be not silly. You're just overcome with all the plans for tomorrow. Why don't you lie down for a short rest?"

"I think I shall. And—and, mother? Did I ever truly say thank you, and that I—love—you—forevermore?" Her voice caught.

Catherine's eyebrows lifted as she smiled. "Verily, Honour, you are a thoughtful daughter. Your actions tell me that every day. Yet your words today are a blessing to me as well. I shall love you to my dying day."

Honour sighed. "Will you tell Molly I am ready for her?"

Catherine nodded, contentment lingering on her lips, and closed the door.

* * *

A church bell, followed by a tap on the door, interrupted Honour's nap. Molly entered the darkened room with a candle and laden trencher.

As the maid curtsied, Honour peeked out of the bed curtains. "What hour is it? Did I rest through the evening meal?"

"That you did. No one wanted to disturb you, with the important day tomorrow. You be needing your sleep to look your best."

As Molly brought the tray and placed it on Honour's lap, the partridge and bread brought back her appetite. And she found herself thirsty for the wine. In mid-gulp, she looked sharply at her maid-friend.

"What hour chimed at the church, Molly?"

"The ninth, methinks." She thought a moment. "Indeed it was. Soon as you eat, I shall brush and braid your hair, then you best return to bed. We all must rise early on the morrow."

Honour picked up the serving of fowl and bit off a piece. She swallowed and reached for the wine glass. With it halfway to her lips, she whispered. "What must I expect of the marriage bed?"

The maid remembered her own young husband, Jack. A smile tugged at the country girl's mouth.

"Ah, Master Dryden will show you—how to please him."

Honour's eyes flashed at Dryden's name. The partridge clattered to the tray and bile rose in her mouth. She touched her lips to wipe them, and a more pleasant memory returned. Richard's touch. The feel of her beloved's lips. Gentle. Pure. Her taut muscles relaxed, and a glowing warmth spread through her.

Blushing as she looked up, Honour steadied her voice. "I—I shall trust the one I love to teach me."

Molly's eyebrows rose at the change in Honour's

demeanor. Then her mouth curved over uneven teeth. "It will go well with you."

Honour's unspoken prayer raced toward the heavens. *Please, God, let it be as she had said, but with Richard and me—tonight!*

The servant stepped to the dressing table.

"Ah—Molly—let us just brush my hair and leave it unbraided."

"Not braid your hair for sleep? You never neglect it! I would be thought remiss in my duties, too. Why ever would you want to do that?"

"I, er, just want to leave it loose tonight."

"It will be a sorry mess tomorrow. How will I ever dress your hair properly if it's full of snarls?" Her voice was puzzled, and her mistress didn't answer.

Honour didn't feel like eating anymore. She motioned for Molly to remove the tray, then moved over in front of the looking glass. The servant began brushing her hair. Honour grew sleepy again, with the maid's gentle, rhythmic strokes. Suddenly, Honour came to herself and realized it had been quite some time since the ninth hour chimed.

"Thank you, Molly. That's all now."

"If you say so, but it could use more, miss."

"I'm very tired. Thank you, and good night."

The moment Molly let herself out of the room, Honour snatched a homespun sack from under the bed. She opened it to pull out her servant's extra dress and shawl, hidden earlier in the day.

Forgive me, Molly, she thought. *Tonight I dare not be discovered.* Then she picked up the jewel box and stared at the Poitier medallion. The gleam of three centuries seemed to mock her betrayal. *Had I a sister, I would leave it for her. But the night's outcome is so uncertain...*

* * *

Part II: Honour

An unexpected rap on the door caused Honour to jump. Before answering, she dropped the disguise onto the bed, drew the curtain, and rapidly set the little chest back over by the fragrance pots.

She drew a breath. "Come in."

"Are you sure you dunna want me to braid your hair?" Molly inquired a final time, wearing her nightdress and cap.

"No! I already told you that!" Struck with a sense of guilt, Honour stretched our her hands toward her girlhood playmate.

"Forgive me. I—I'm not quite myself tonight. Molly, you really are a dear. You may not know how much I depend on you." Honour grasped her maid's hand.

"Why, 'tis all right. I help you gladly."

"God bless you, Molly."

"Good night."

As Honour put on the servant's clothes, she fastened the brooch to her underclothing and thought of all the brides who had worn the medallion before her. The tenth hour chimed. While she listened for the quiet of sleep to fall upon Mayfield Hall, Honour prayed that her mother would forgive.

* * *

Richard cautiously slowed his fatigued mount to a walk as he approached the manor stables. The soldier's ears strained for signs of unusual activity this night, but all they heard was muted animal noise. His hand unconsciously touched the pouch carrying the vital document he had secured in London, and the circle of silver for his bride.

It had been a harrowing trip along pathetic, little-used tracks through one restless village after another. He only hoped that he arrived in time, that Honour wasn't already in Dryden's clutches. He wondered how effectively Edward had been able to shield the plans from discovery.

If I am here in time, all the hiding in the woods and dodging Parliamentarians and highwaymen was worth the effort. If not... He frowned in the dark. *I cannot bear to think of Honour's ultimate fate.*

Richard shook his curly head. *Banish those thoughts and get on with it, man!*

The Cavalier's booted feet glided smoothly from the stirrups to the damp cobblestones below. In only a few strides, he nearly crossed the courtyard.

"Blast!" Richard ground out the word, recovering his balance from a sudden collision with the sundial at the opposite edge of the yard. A bridle-weary hand rubbed at his hip. He took advantage of the pause to listen again intently. Satisfied again, the soldier strode through the stone archway, meeting up with the path to the dairy barn.

* * *

In that same building's tiny loft, Fanny sat bolt upright on the straw mattress. She clapped her hand suddenly to her mouth. In her dream, the head dairyman had her to himself again, and...

Fanny's eyes widened in true fright. *Oh, no, he said if I didn't take care of that sick calf this evening, he'd whip and use me again.*

She moaned quietly, while she reached for her own threadbare shawl and poked a strand of lifeless hair back into her dirty night cap. *I hope the animal isn't dead!*

Her mind returned to that bloody night just passed, when her actions almost let the new creature leave this world before it arrived.

"Stupid, clumsy idiot," he had said. Well, she had not meant to damage the young thing struggling to be born. Truly. Just nothing lately ever turned out right, since he started making her sleep all alone in the barn and came in

Part II: Honour

the night to hurt her. At least he hadn't come tonight. *But if that calf be dead...*

A bare foot tentatively felt for the top rung of the ladder. She then descended rapidly, landing with a soft jump to the familiar dirt floor.

Fanny's preoccupied mind didn't register the first muffled sound. But when a latch squeaked in the quiet, the back of her neck prickled. Without even thinking, Fanny ducked into an empty cattle crib. Pulse pounded in her temples and her teeth chattered, in spite of the relative warmth inside the barn.

Startled to hear the soft footfalls of several people instead of her single dreaded visitor, she peeked curiously between the crude slats that protected her from discovery. Her teeth ceased chattering. *Surely these intruders mean no harm, whatever their strange errand.*

A stooped form slipped in the great door, his long robes dragging the hard-packed earth. As the figure struck a flint and a candle sputtered to life, a fringe of silver hair and heavy cross caught the light.

Mother of God, what has the old vicar to do with this place?

Just then two young men appeared in the doorway. Fanny wiggled, crouching even lower to peer through a slightly wider opening. The men exchanged a few words in whispers, one bending very close to his elder's head.

A rolled document passed noiselessly from one Cavalier's hands to the ancient servant of God. After passing the candle to the shorter soldier, the vicar's tremory hands uncurled the parchment and looked up at the taller of the two.

"The license appears to be in order, my son. But—where is she?"

* * *

Honour's slippered feet padded quietly out the door of her own room, along the main corridor in the direction of the servants' stair. A homespun shawl covered her heavy hair. *'Tis so dark. If I'm seen in this simple gown, someone will take me for a servant, I pray.*

The huge sandstone house settled with a loud creak as she reached the stair. Honour paused and held her breath. Then she crept toward the main floor.

She continued down the stairs until she reached the main floor, then turned toward the hall beside the grand staircase. Lingering briefly in the shadows to watch, she traversed the short space to the breakfast room door, unbolted it, and flung it open. Hardly noticing the lake straight ahead, she turned her face toward their meeting place. When her feet hit the soft grass, she broke into a run and crossed the upper field. The closer her steps took her to the dairy barn, the faster her feet flew.

Turning her ankle slightly in a cow track, she slowed momentarily and put her hand to her heaving chest.

She felt the medallion through Molly's dress. *Let Richard be there!* her heart cried.

With renewed urgency, she raced ahead. Honour's midnight tresses streamed out behind her in the sweet scented air, only partly obscured by the coarse shawl and gown that billowed behind her.

As she reached the barn, the wary girl paused to catch her breath. She leaned against the door and listened. *Richard!* Reassured by the soft murmur of her beloved's voice, she resolutely slipped inside, closing the door behind her.

Her eyes searched for his in the flickering candlelight.

"G—God be with you."

"And also with you." Her breath caught on the familiar greeting, and a pulse hammered at her throat.

* * *

Part II: Honour

Richard silently reached out his arms to the woman he loved. As he clasped her against the muscular length of his body, he closed his eyes and felt the thudding of Honour's heart through the coarse dress.

Suddenly, an image of Honour in true bridal attire flitted across his mind. He'd heard talk of the expensive silk dress, beaded with pearl, and the lace cap all the villagers expected her to wear on the morrow. Pure and beautiful—and yoked with the wrong husband.

Richard's muscles tensed, and he tightened his grasp on Honour. In a moment, he loosed her enough to turn her ivory face and shoulders toward the bent old man. "We must hasten to do this."

"May the God Almighty bless you, my children, and may He dismiss any deception employed on this holy, but unusual, occasion." The trusted vicar's aged eyes needed no book to follow, and thus he began the costly deed.

"In the name of the Father and the Son and the Holy Ghost, amen. Do you, er, Richard Clayton Allen, take this woman.... Do you, Honour Elizabeth Mayfield, take this man....?"

In the distance, the village church bell tolled the eleventh hour.

"What God hath joined together, let no man put asunder!"

Hastily, the grayed churchman reached inside his robes for a quill and scratched a signature at the bottom of the license. As he began to roll it up again, a raucous noise split the air just outside. The four candlelit faces froze.

Drunken boasting echoed against the building's stone walls, as a huge body thumped against the closed door.

* * *

Circle of Love

Fanny cringed. Rivers of ice ran suddenly in her fingers. She knew that voice. Still rooted to her hiding place, she couldn't help but watch the drama unfolding before her incredulous eyes.

* * *

Richard grasped the rolled parchment and crammed it into the ugly crock he'd found to protect it. Taking the unsteady candle from his beloved's hands, the bridegroom began to melt a waxen seal around the opening. Honour brushed against him. Her ring fell into the straw, and she dropped to her knees in search.

Meaty fists banged on the bolted door of the barn. And with the noise came angry shouts.

The candle went out. In the pitch darkness, feet tangled as the furtive group lunged for a low doorway at the rear of the barn. Somehow, in the jostle and confusion, the precious container slipped from Richard's hands, thudded to the earthen floor and clinked against a hard wall. Just as the huge main door swung open.

The bridegroom paused just long enough to weigh the decision—reach for the proof, or flee—before he and the others plunged through the small door into the barnyard.

* * *

With sweat beaded on her forehead, Fanny waited, extremely still. The clumsy dairyman staggered into the space occupied moments before by the secret drama. He muttered and swore. As Fanny heard her name hurled out of his mouth again and again, she cowered deeper into the stall. The oaf mounted the ladder to her sleep loft and cursed even louder when he found it empty. After spending his wrath destroying the straw mattress and the dairy maid's

Part II: Honour

scant belongings, the tyrant stumbled back down the ladder and out the way he had come in.

Several minutes later, Fanny crept out of her hiding place. Curiosity fueled her search. Finding a candle stub and flint in the loft, she retrieved the crockery and searched frantically for the ring. At last, her fingers closed around it. Torn by her need to escape the manor, and her loyalty to the young mistress, she made an important choice. In the barn, she found a digging implement. Completing the seal, the milk maid—who never before seemed to do anything right—dug a deep hole in the earth and secreted the Rhenish crock. Intently, she performed the strange task, without ever knowing the value of her actions.

* * *

Following the swift exit to the barnyard, the players in the wedding drama separated in two different directions. Edward and the old vicar took a seldom-used path that wound back toward the church. Richard clutched Honour's hand so tightly it hurt, as they slipped warily back across the uneven field. Within sight of the house, the husband abruptly turned south, toward the lower end of the small lake where the waiting horse was tethered. Honour unconsciously resisted him and looked back toward her family home.

Richard pulled her into a clump of trees along the shore. They stood a moment in the dark. Honour reached for the object hidden in her clothes. She unlatched the brooch and brought it forth for her husband's fingers to trace. "For nearly 300 years brides of our family have worn this on their wedding day."

"As you have done this night." He felt the heraldic design raised from the heavy golden surface.

"Beside you, this is all I have—now," she breathed shakily. "Well, Snowflake, too."

"And, most of all, God. Mistress Allen—I shall like calling you that—always remember He goes with us." Richard ran his thumb across the embossed brooch once more. "Here, let me replace it for you." His large hands fumbled against her soft skin.

Black water of the narrow lake lapped gently. Richard sniffed. Something ominous mingled with the breeze.

Chapter Eighteen

Edward chopped away brambles that tangled over the path, impeding their progress. The old priest tripped and caught himself against a tree trunk. Finally, they reached a place where the path joined with another, and the way grew easier, smoother. But they were more exposed. The grizzled one murmured a prayer for the young couple, then said to Edward, "After entry in the parish register, I can lower these bones into my bed once more."

Sudden outcries sounded back near the manor. Edward's skin prickled as he tried to look through the trees. "I am loathe to leave you without escort, old sir..."

"Nay. I shall find my way home from here. From the church 'tis only steps to my bed."

"I must return to the troops. Surely the Roundheads attack not this night, but even so my blood runs cold at yonder sounds."

"Go on with you. No one will find fault with a bent old priest such as I."

* * *

An acrid smell mingled with the pine and yew. Richard wondered, *Pitch?* To the east he glimpsed through the trees the orange of torches against the sky. Then he heard it: the rattle of swords and hoofbeats. Quickly they grew closer, and distinguishable shouts rang through the air.

"Vengeance on the Royalists!"

"Unseat the tyrant on the throne!"

The most strident curdled his blood. "Burn Mayfield Manor!"

Of their own accord, Captain Allen's deft hands found the hilt of his sword. Just before he rushed out of the shadows, he checked his reaction. Every inch of his body poised for the confrontation, as he'd trained himself and the soldiers in his command.

But this night! In a flash of torches had he forgotten the new bonds just forged? What of the pledge to lay aside the encumbrances of the past and follow the uncharted course? The spiritual war, his conflicting loyalties, tore at his deepest insides.

Jaws clenched, neck muscles corded, Richard pulled his bride against his body. *Honour! My love!* His spirit weighed the choices and it became clear. For the first time in Richard's adult life, proving himself on the battlefield must take second place. Only minutes ago, this girl-woman had placed her entire life in his hands. Even betraying his presence at this moment could jeopardize her future and place her back under Dryden's malevolent control. A battlefield death now would be the cruelest betrayal of love imaginable. And a sensual corollary coursed through his mind: a valiant—but fallen—Cavalier could never experience the full charms of his bride.

Better to suffer the wrath of King Charles himself... The implication struck him like a blow to the chest. Now there would be no possibility of coming back—for either of them. *A deserter and a runaway. The Virginia Colony becomes*

Part II: Honour

our only choice.

A servant's desperate screams cut through the air. "Awake! Awake!"

Honour shivered; she stared openmouthed at the spectacle.

Multiple human shapes staggered out of the imposing manor and scattered in the direction of the various outbuildings. As the raiders grew closer to the house, she whispered, "No! No! No!" And she tried to break free of her husband's grasp.

Richard's arms held her as bands of iron. His heart suffered in silent anguish, as he drew Honour deeper under cover of an ancient spreading fir. They watched the coming confrontation well hidden, in a natural room curtained with evergreen lace that draped to the ground.

Of all those who had lodged under the manor roof, Lady Catherine emerged last. Circled by a troop of Cavaliers, swords drawn, she stood her ground before the line of Roundheads. In the torchlight, dignity showed in her bearing as she faced their leader.

Captain Barbour's voice carried across the grassy slope. "In the name of Parliament, Lady Mayfield." He nodded toward the authorization in his hand. "Your holdings are to be burned, for continued loyalty to the Crown."

"May I be assured of safety for my family, and our servants and tenants?" The widow's voice was surprisingly strong enough to carry across the small lake.

"Only if they lay down their arms and remain in the church until our task is complete. I promise you safe conduct there, upon my personal word as a gentleman. Now, hand over the keys."

Catherine lifted her chin defiantly. "I require an armed escort of his Majesty's soldiers to the church." But the rattle of keys betrayed the shaking of her hand as she touched them on her girdle. "That is, if you wish the master keys."

"'Twould make the task cleaner, Lady Catherine," he admitted. "Very well, a contingent shall escort your people to the church, provided it remains with you there until our work is finished." He paused. "I have no quarrel with you personally. My orders are to reduce the assets of the Crown."

Barbour adjusted this helmet and reached for the keys.

* * *

Catherine looked round the tight knot of people. *Where is Honour?* Her search landed on a cloaked figure she assumed was her daughter. *How I long for Honour's support at this moment, but I greatly fear to draw attention to her.*

The Royalist forces formed a ring of protection around them. She relinquished the keys. And the lady and her household began the mile march to sanctuary in the church.

* * *

Honour and Richard soon lost sight of Catherine and the servants, winding down the pathway to the village.

Captain Barbour shouted, "Burn all the outbuildings, but save the main house until I examine the estate's papers." Then he disappeared through the massive front door.

The young bride could no longer choke back her sobs.

Richard grasped her by the shoulders. "We must make our escape, now, while the troops are occupied. Else we are undone! Wait here."

While he strode farther into the trees to loose Snowflake's tether, Honour stood mesmerized by the scene before her. A ghastly orange circle flared across the Mayfield lands, as the first outbuildings winked with flame. Honour's shoulders shook, and teardrops coursed down her pale cheeks.

Richard untied the horse, and drew a lump of charcoal

Part II: Honour

from his purse to cover Snowflake's white marking. "Discovery now means death," he murmured, rubbing the horse's face.

As he returned to Honour's side, he heard the roar. One structure after another surrendered to the awful crackling and splitting of the fire. "They didn't have to do that, the cruel swine." He looked back down at the ground, and swallowed hard.

He lifted his eyes. Between the burning hay ricks on the hill, he saw the dairy barn catch.

His heart did a somersault. *The ring. The license.* Dropped in their flight. All proof of their marriage now engulfed in a conflagration. Unless the priest could enter the union in the register before Lady Catherine and the household sought sanctuary there.

* * *

Edward ran down the village road toward Mayfield Hall. But he had only traveled past the first curve, when he came face to face with Lady Catherine, her servants, and his own troops, most of them on foot. And behind them the sinister torches of the Roundheads.

He spun round and fell in step beside the gentlewoman. She explained rapidly what had transpired only moments earlier. "Let them destroy my goods, if they must, as long as they preserve our lives." Edward marveled at the strength in her voice, as they approached the lych-gate of the church.

Then Catherine stumbled and would have fallen, had Edward not caught her. They stopped abruptly. A crumpled form lay at their feet—an old man in a priest's robe, fresh blood oozing from his temple.

"Father!" Edward knelt by his side and lifted the battered head. "Oh, dear God, who could be so wicked?"

The old man's lips moved. "Forgive them....Round..."

He struggled to say more. "The register. Not... yet... writ... in the register." His eyes focused briefly on Catherine, then his body slumped and his last word ended with a gurgle. "Honour."

Catherine's hand fled to her throat. "Honour!" In a panic, she searched the faces gathered around. Her daughter's was not among them. She reached out to the hooded figure she'd seen earlier and whirled her around. It was Molly.

"Molly, Edward, where is Honour? Have you seen her?" The servant girl's face froze in fear. "I made certain her— her bed was empty before I fled the house. I beg you to believe me."

Edward and another Cavalier lifted the priest's body and carried him toward the church. "Make haste! Gather everyone inside!" He groaned under the weight—both of the old man and the news he must tell Catherine. But he stalled for time, that Richard might yet steal Honour away. "I will explain when all are safe inside."

The Mayfield folk huddled together while two officers lit candles on the altar. Eerie shadows snaked along the walls.

Edward and the other man laid the priest in front of the choir screen. In a rush of emotion, he drew his sword and charged back out the main door, straight into the face of the Roundheads. Catherine followed him, but his sleeve slipped from her grasp.

"Have you no respect for a man of the cloth?" he shouted on the stone steps. "May you rot in hell, murderers!" Edward slashed at the torchbearers, and six were on him in a moment.

Catherine stood back in horror as a blade ran the lieutenant through and the breath of life escaped his body. She knelt beside him, while the Parliament forces drew back among the gravestones. "You cannot die until you tell me!" she shrieked. "Where is Honour? Oh, where is my daughter?"

But Edward's lips, twisted in pain, were forever silent.

* * *

Honour and Richard picked their way through the night shadows along the road. Little help came from the waning moon. At daybreak, they came upon a place where a lake hugged the left side of the track, while on the right lay a soft, green slope carpeted in ferns. The hardwoods grew close by the road, exposed roots nearly forming a ladder to the land below. The couple dismounted, to give Snowflake a rest from their weight, and walked toward the cover of the trees.

Honour stumbled, and Richard caught her. They embraced. For a long moment, they gathered strength from one another.

"We must stop and rest." He guided her down the slope.

She could barely nod in the early light.

The bridegroom spread his traveling cloak on the mossy earth. Then he gently helped his bride lie down and stretched out beside her. Honour's head lay against his heart, with his shoulder as a pillow.

Fatigued as he was, he could not resist touching her. His fingers traced the smooth skin down the hollow of her throat. He drew aside the brown homespun she wore and traced the shape of the brooch hidden on her chemise. Then his right hand strayed further to brush her soft skin.

She felt the hammering of his heart but could not help herself. Her weary body stiffened and for the first time ever, she drew away from his touch. "Please..."

He leaned over her. "I know 'tis not the finest inn, but this is all I have to offer you."

Honour shut her eyes and turned her head from side to side. "'Tisn't that." She reached out a shaking hand toward his face. And soon the trembling took over her whole self.

Circle of Love

Richard stroked her hair and turned her toward his chest. Close but undemanding, he kneaded the tightness in her back and silently cursed the terrors stalking them both. When she finally slept, he gazed at her innocent features and wondered when he would truly know his bride. *Please, Father, grant patience, and preserve our lives this day, and the next, and the next...*

* * *

When the sun reached noon height, they awoke and moved on, following the road but ready to hide in the woods at a moment's notice.

Snowflake's ears pricked, and presently the humans also heard the clinking and squeaking of a group of horsemen.

"Armed, by the sound of them." Richard dismounted and led Snowflake down the tricky slope to the woodland floor.

Scarcely had they hidden in the trees and undergrowth before a small contingent of Roundheads—heavily armed—pounded past on the roadway above.

As the sound of hooves echoed in the distance, Richard gathered his bride in his arms. She fit there so well, so warmly. His stubbly cheek grazed the rough fiber of her servant clothing.

"Someday," he vowed, "I wish to clothe you in proper raiment—to show your true beauty..."

"Being with you in rags is preferable to the nuptial gown—and all others—left behind, my love." She tentatively reached a hand and stroked the coarse whiskers along his jaw. Her voice was almost inaudible. "I am—sorry for being so afraid."

* * *

Part II: Honour

Snowflake picked her way along the underbrush, within sight of the main road, yet hidden. Richard and Honour walked ahead, leading the horse. They approached a stream.

A flurry of hooves pounded in the distance. Then the small band of riders grew nearer and nearer.

Instinctively, the secret travelers drew farther into the wood and stopped.

Suddenly, the hoofbeats ceased, close-by. The riders made no effort to cloak their noise as they dismounted and crashed through the brush, tracing the path of the stream. One came exceedingly close to their hiding place, where he relieved himself.

Snowflake sniffed the air and whinnied, then pulled against her lead.

"Someone goes there." The leader of the band drew his weapons, and his followers did the same. They encircled the sound, then worked their way inward as toward the hub of a carriage wheel.

Richard lowered Honour to the ground and straddled her form with his long legs. His rapier ready, he twisted this way and that against the approaching attackers.

A pistol glinted in the daylight, dangerously close.

Richard called out, "What do you want?"

"Aye. A smart man, that. Why, we wants your purse—all of it." The highwayman swaggered as he came into view.

"Then come no closer. I shall toss it to you. I have none else. You can trust the saints on it." Richard tightened the purse strings, then let it go.

The leather pouch fell near the leader's feet. He snatched it up with a gloved hand. The gold coins the soldier had saved from the last of his pay clinked in the pouch.

The robbers rode off with a shout of triumph. Richard and Honour had escaped with their lives, but the passage money was gone.

Chapter Nineteen

A thatched-roof inn came into view as the couple rounded a curve on the narrow track.

"News of London reaches here with regularity. I must inquire as to the general situation of things." Richard spoke thus as he halted their progress and drew into cover of the wood. He dismounted.

Gently, he reached for Honour's waist and eased her to the ground. As he placed the reins in her hands, their eyes met. He saw both fear and trust mingled there. Her mouth moved as if to voice a question. Quickly, he planted a kiss on her lips, removing his plumed hat.

"Remain hidden." He paused. "Watch and pray."

Cautiously, Richard made his way toward the inn. Not wanting to attract undue attention, he slipped into the stable area, avoiding the main door.

A man shoveled muck from the stalls.

"Hear ye any news from London?"

The man just grunted.

"I say, any couriers through here lately from the south?"

Reluctantly, the stabler turned from his work and leaned on his smelly tool. "Aye. And what would ye be knowing for?"

"Something to occupy my thoughts, 'tis all. Wonder how the King and his enemies be fighting."

"One of Parliament's regiments passed this way nigh unto three days ago. Laughing, they was to tell of happenings, and gone right back to London to celebrate."

"Go on."

"One of 'em tells me that dandy Prince Rupert slipped up on Brentford under cover of mist and took the town. But Essex got over the Chiltern Hills first and battled him at Turnham Green. I heard it were 24,000 of them Londoners what faced down the King. To hear them tell it, his Majesty and his lesser thousands tucked tail and went back to lick their wounds at Oxford." He stabbed the shovel into the ground and, turning his back to Richard, reached up to adjust a harness hanging on the wall. "But me, I jest try to do me job and let them high-borns fight it out."

Richard felt a weight on his chest, a sudden loss of ability to take in air.

"Guess that makes London more a Parliament town than ever..." the stabler babbled on—to an empty room.

Richard had disappeared.

* * *

Not an hour later, a gray-haired nobleman barked at the same stabler, "Here! Tend the horse and be quick about it, while I go inside for a drink." With a pronounced limp, he walked round to the inn door.

When the man returned, he mounted the horse and stopped under the stable door. Casually, as if an afterthought, he turned to the groom and asked, "Anyone else come through today on horseback?"

The servant paused with a pail of oats in his hands. "Just a lone soldier. Long, light hair. Been on the road awhile, by

Part II: Honour

the looks of him. Dunno what direction he be traveling."

Scudamore grinned. "You have been most helpful. Good day." He gave the horse a vicious kick and galloped south.

* * *

The quay at Southampton teemed with carts and wagons piled with goods. People swarmed the gangplanks. Smells of fish and saltwater, mingled with the general commotion, frightened Honour, who had never been this far away from the manor. She clung more tightly to Richard's middle. Snowflake showed signs of weariness, and her white blaze peeked through the smears of charcoal.

Honour's stomach rumbled and she swayed sideways, almost losing her balance. Perspiration rose on her brow. *How long has it been since the villager in Cricklade shared her meagre rations with us? These last two days without money or food feel more like two weeks!*

They had been on the run for five days in all. Her maid's clothing, caked with dust and sweat, hung stiffly on her frame.

If only Richard still carried his purse! We'd not have had to beg bread from out-of-the-way folks—for fear of discovery. Dryden may even now be in pursuit of us! Her eyes darted, searching the crowd for his malevolent face.

But she still had her beloved. *'Twas far better to satisfy the highwaymen with his purse than his blood.*

She looked at the shipping offices, a line of low stone buildings at the quay.

What other hope lay open for a soldier—nay, a deserter—of the King's Cavaliers, encumbered with his girl-bride of five days, hunted by a spurned betrothed?

Some distance ahead of them, a man alighted from a hired carriage and snarled a command to the driver. The nobleman's back was turned as he walked into the furthest shipping office.

Honour drew in her breath sharply. "Richard." Her whisper was urgent. "Richard, that man limps like Dryden!"

Richard reigned Snowflake abruptly and plunged into a narrow space between buildings. He dismounted without a word and helped Honour down. Then he tied up the horse. "Wait for him to get inside the shipping company," Richard said. The couple paused in the semi-darkness.

Honour placed a hand over her heart. For the first time in several days she became conscious of the brooch hidden there. She touched it again through the rough blouse, her hands trembling at the implications of her idea. She considered their situation, at the edge of the sea without the passage money in Richard's purse. And the likelihood of Dryden being so near.

Honour swallowed hard, then spun around to face her beloved. "I have the answer!" Her speech was hurried and breathless. "We shall sell the brooch for our passage money..."

Richard grasped her hand. "No! How can we sell the Poitier piece entrusted to your keeping by your family?"

Her voice was firm. "And how shall a childless bride pass it on to her heir, if the bride perishes at the pier or is carried home in disgrace? Of what use is it then?" She pulled away from Richard and started toward the street.

He caught up with her and shoved her into the first doorway.

A middle-aged man looked up from a table littered with lists. "Amos McConnell, the Levant Company." From beneath bushy eyebrows, he studied the disheveled pair. "What can I do for ye today?"

Honour and Richard spoke at the same time. "How much is passage to the Virginia Colony?"

The man leaned back in his chair. "And when would ye be goin'?"

"As soon as possible." Richard straightened, as if to shift the burden of responsibility on his shoulders.

"Could be yer in luck. The *Sunrise* sails fer Jamestown at the next tide, but she's amighty full up. Unexpected it is to be sending a ship this late in the season, but the recent harvest by the James River was meagre at best. The settlers have bad need for supplies to see them through winter."

Honour looked the man straight in the eye. "We must be on the ship tonight."

"And what betakes you to the wilds of Virginia?" The man of commerce shifted his gaze to Richard. "What do ye do for a livin'? Have ye a land grant from the King?"

Honour and Richard looked at one another. Then the young husband tried to smooth his sleeve. "I—I am..."

"Thou looks..."

Richard interrupted in a rush. "I am a teacher, sir, educated in Latin, Greek and history."

"Thou looks every inch a soldier to me, one of the King's Cavaliers."

"My father distinguished himself in the Irish Rebellion and gave his life for the King, while I pursued priestly studies."

The older man chuckled. "And found such a beautiful lass captive in a musty library of ancient manuscripts, no doubt."

Honour looked over at Richard, a shy smile on her face.

"Well, almost." Then her features tightened again. "Truly, sir, if we may sail tonight, tell us the cost."

"I take it you have no land charter."

"None, sir." Richard lifted his hands, palms up. "But I have these strong hands to work and knowledge to share."

"Have you the five pounds required for passage?"

Honour turned her back and fiddled with her maid's clothing. She unclasped the brooch and held it out. Her hand shook. "Thanks to highwaymen along the Oxford road, no.

But this ancient piece..." She hesitated. *Forgive me, Mother.*

The man's eyebrows lifted, even as he rose from his chair to lean over the table. "May I see it?" He took it from her and turned it over and over in his hands, feeling the weight and evaluating the craftsmanship. "'Tis a significant piece of work, almost enough for your voyage. Have ye anythin' else?"

"My—my horse is tethered outside. A Barbary mare of fine build. She stands a full fifteen hands high." Honour winced as she considered the inevitable parting from her Snowflake.

"Mind if I have a look?"

Honour nodded painfully as Amos went out for a brief inspection. As he led the horse out of the alley into better light, a man of grim expression and stringy hair walked past and ducked into a doorway. He stared covertly at Amos and the mare, because of its smudged marking on the face. With a knowing expression in his mismatched eyes, the watcher patted a pearl-handled pistol and blended into the shadows—to wait.

Amos returned, satisfied with the value of the horseflesh and unmindful of anything amiss. He gave the couple a benign smile. Then as he dropped the Poitier brooch into his purse, Amos thought of his old friend, the master jeweler up north who would want to study its intricacies of design. "I shall pay the stutterer a visit in a fortnight," he murmured to himself.

The man sat down again at his desk and reached for the passenger list. He turned it toward the bride and handed her a quill to make a mark. She wrote her new name—Honour Mayfield Allen—in fluid script, then passed the quill to Richard.

The shipper cleared his throat as he directed his attention to the young man. "And what have ye for yer passage?"

Richard's fingers tightened around the quill. "The

medallion and steed ought to be enough for both."

Amos shook his gray head. "Nay. The brooch is naught of sufficient weight to offset thine aboard my ship. And the horse, though well-bred, is nearly lame."

A look of panic passed between the pair, and Honour gripped Richard's hand to summon strength. "You dishonour my ancestors, sir. 'Tis obviously an ancient piece. And the horse, a gift of my beloved father. He died at Edgehill." She gave McConnell a piercing look, even as her heart despaired.

A door opened behind them, and Honour let out a cry. Richard grasped her firmly at the waist and whirled round to face the intruder. Then as suddenly as he grabbed her, the soldier relaxed his grip.

It was not Dryden who entered but, rather, a stranger to them both.

Yet not to Amos. The shipper nearly jumped from behind his desk. "Samuel!" He clapped the man on the back. "And how be Alice and the expected bairn?"

The brown-haired man in his thirties looked right past Honour and Richard, dismissing the travel-worn pair as soldier and tavern maid. His lips tried to smile at his jovial friend, but they could not. "Alice took to her bed five days ago, though she moves around the room today. 'Twas a difficult time, and despite my medical knowledge, I couldn't get him breathing. Our...our boy babe was too early." He looked downcast as he brushed his hat on the knee of his pants. "I laid him in the churchyard yesterday."

Amos shook his head in sympathy. "The Lord wrap His arms round ye in comfort, as surely as He cradles your wee lamb." With a gentle hand on Sneade's arm, he continued, "Yer little family's place is yet reserved on the *Sunrise*, but you'll not be sailing this evening now, I'm certain."

"Exactly what I came to see you about, Amos. We dare not wait till spring to get a physician to the settlement. Alice swears she is fit enough and can gather her strength nearly as well on shipboard as on land. But there is still one impediment. With my son William only ten years old, I need a manservant to help clear land and build a house in the settlement. And none have I found these days, with my wife and babe in travail."

Amos looked over toward Richard and Honour, a question on his face.

Richard stepped forward and spoke to Samuel. It was a firm voice for one in such crusty clothing. "Richard Allen at your service, sir."

Samuel turned in confusion to his friend Amos, then to the soldier. "Samuel Sneade." He looked Richard over, from the torn lace on his collar to his mud-encrusted boots. "How does one of his Majesty's—er—officers propose to assist me?"

Richard swallowed. "I wish to become indentured to you, sir, in return for paying my passage to the Virginia Colony."

Honour clasped her hands behind her. Her nails dug into the white flesh. She opened her mouth to speak but no sound came.

"Why are you not battling the Roundheads? I heard mention of you during the royal visit to High House." Pride expanded his chest. "King Charles made my cousin Ralph a colonel there."

Richard stepped closer to Samuel and leaned to his ear. "My bride and I seek refuge from a black-hearted scoundrel just paces down this very street. Dryden Scudamore," he whispered.

Samuel spoke aloud. "The cur of Staffordshire? My relations told me the story."

Honour didn't even try to keep the hard edge out of her voice. "The same."

"What happenstance brought you here?"

Richard said, "For all my service to the King, I possess no land grant, like yours. I spirited my bride away in the thick of battle, highwaymen robbed us, and our only friend in high places languishes in the Tower. We stand on the edge of disaster, sir. I beg you to make me your servant."

"But to indenture a man the likes of you, a near equal—'tis unthinkable!"

Richard squared his shoulders. "In all due respect, sir, it is unthinkable to stay here. Honour's passage is paid by her only personal possessions, but I cannot bear to send her to the wilds alone."

Samuel looked thoughtful. "I agonized when it appeared I'd lose my Alice a'birthing these past days, in spite of my training. Burying the babe is hurt enough."

Samuel scuffed his boot against the floor. "My conscience does not wish me to bind you formally for a period of years."

"I insist, sir, on paying my debt. And presently the sweat of my brow is the only means I have."

Honour's eyes widened in wonder, as she witnessed again the costly love Richard held for her. She reached out her hands and stepped forward, more aware than ever of her lowly attire. "Kind sir, I would gladly serve your wife on the voyage and beyond. With her poor health and your boy William, she will need an attendant..."

Samuel scrutinized the pair. "How do I know you are not lovers running together in sin, destined for the judgment of God?" His glance fell on Honour's ringless fingers and rose to her pale face. Certainly her well-kept hands and high-born speech disqualified her as a common waif. "Have you a certificate of marriage?"

Richard looked at him steadily. "No, sir. We fled from the Roundheads after repeating our vows in secret, under special license from the Archbishop of Canterbury—God preserve him. Our certificate of marriage perished in the flames." He brightened with confidence. "Yet the parish register bears us witness."

"I accept your word for now, Richard Allen," said Samuel. "But I shall also send inquiry this night to confirm your statement. The Ten Commandments are kept in my home." He pointed a finger at the couple. "Should news reach me in the New World your marriage is false, dishonour shall rain upon your head. I shall cast out your woman and any bastards born to you. And you shall labor more than the full term of your servitude. Is that understood?"

Richard and Honour nodded gravely.

Amos cleared his throat in the awkward silence. "Shall I draw up the indenture document, my friends?"

"Very well," said Samuel, as he pulled out a chair and sat down.

Richard bent over to add his name below Honour's to the passenger list.

* * *

Samuel straightened after signing the indenture document. "Now, Richard Allen, return with me to my lodgings and we shall bring the wife and son to the ship."

Honour stood on tiptoe to speak in her husband's ear. "I shall accompany you, but first let me claim our bundle upon Snowflake, and—and bid her goodbye."

He turned and saw her chin quiver, then set itself firm again. Richard put his hand in hers and led her to follow Samuel.

A few feet ahead, Samuel lifted the latch and swung the door on its rusty hinges. Then he stepped back suddenly, trouncing Richard's boots, and shut the door in haste.

"Flee to the back room." The urgency in his voice was clear as he motioned to the pair. "And I shall depart the rear—alone. A man stands in the shadows, a firearm in his jerkin."

He glanced at Amos as an afterthought. His friend nodded. "They shall remain here with me until you return. By then, a copy of the manifest will be ready for your delivery to the captain."

As Samuel scrambled out the back way, Amos bolted the main door then led Honour and Richard to a small storeroom. He lit a candle, settled them on the floor, and brought them a bite to eat. "Rest. I'll light a lamp and be copyin' the ships documents until Samuel returns."

Honour spoke tentatively. "Have you tended to the horse, sir?"

"I shall." He nodded as he answered.

"Might you fetch our bundle as well?" she ventured.

"Of course."

Long before the lone candle guttered, the exhausted couple had drifted into a disturbed sleep.

* * *

Honour sat up in the dark, leaning on one elbow. "Richard," she whispered.

He opened gritty eyes but couldn't see her form. "Yes, Honour."

"What if—just what if the old priest did not make straight for the church register? The smell of war was all around us. What if the Roundheads did not leave him alone and there stands no marriage recorded at Keele?"

He came upright and ran his hands through his tangled hair. "I pray never, ever to be separated from you. But as Jacob of the Hebrews served seven years—plus seven—for his beloved Rachael, surely I can endure a shorter servitude for you." He reached out in the blackness and folded her hand in his. "God is our witness. It is in His hands."

Scarce had the words left his mouth, when the two heard

Circle of Love

a team of horses and rapid footsteps. The storeroom door opened. Samuel and Amos each extended a hand, but Richard and Honour were already on their feet.

Samuel leaned close to speak, while Richard buckled on his sheathed rapier. "I fear this building is yet being watched. A coach waits outside bearing my wife and son. It is drawn up close to the door. Make haste! The ship waits but shall weigh anchor in little more than a quarter hour."

In an instant, Honour bundled the remains of their bread, and followed the men to the door. Amos unbolted it, gave Sneade the shipping documents, and placed his hand on Samuel's arm.

"Godspeed, my friend."

"Godspeed." Samuel flung open the door, pushed Honour and Richard into the coach, and fell in behind them, slamming the door shut. At once, the driver urged the horses down the cobblestone street toward the *Sunrise*. Inside, Mr. Sneade tersely introduced his family to the newcomers of their party.

At the wharf, Samuel turned to his manservant. "Richard, I sent our trunks ahead. You and the girl wait in the coach until Dame Alice and William board ship. My driver will stay with you." He climbed out quickly and reached to help his wife and son. They started up the gangplank. She stumbled on a loose board and Samuel steadied her.

Honour peered through a crack between the window curtains. "They are safely aboard. Let's go." She squeezed his hand hard.

Richard rose and opened the door of the coach. He moved swiftly to help Honour down. The moment he set her feet on the cobblestones, the door slammed against his shoulders and he felt stale breath against his neck. As the barrel of a wheel-lock pistol nudged the Cavalier's back, he flung her toward the gangplank, yelling, "Honour, run! Run for the ship!"

A strong arm grabbed for Honour and ripped her sleeve. But she tore free. The same claws then caught Richard around the middle and whirled him around. He saw a twisted visage of profound wickedness.

"Damn you to hell! You stole my bride." Palpable hatred flashed in Dryden Scudamore's strange eyes.

And for the first time Richard stood toe to toe with the renegade noble who spoiled everything his crafty hands touched. Fear for Honour's safety, and even his own, mingled in Richard's heart with the satisfaction of facing his personal enemy.

Dryden's mismatched eyes burned with a lust for revenge. His thin lips stretched over rotten teeth in a leer of triumph, as he rammed the barrel of the gun against Richard's breastbone.

"*'To me belongeth vengeance,'* saith the Lord. *'...for the day of their calamity is at hand.'*" Richard gasped the holy words in pain, as Scudamore pressed the pistol harder against the young soldier's chest.

Dryden spat at him. "Not this time..."

The younger man brought his elbows up quickly, and there came a bright flash and a plume of smoke. Richard reeled backwards. He felt intense burning—somewhere above his heart—but still on his feet, he plunged up the gangplank.

Dryden cursed bitterly as he fumbled to reload the dueling piece. "Death is too good for you, Richard Allen!"

As his boots struck the first crossbar, Richard screamed at the small knot of people at the ship's rail just ahead of him. "Get down!" He charged toward the place where they hid, then turned round, making certain Honour was well behind him. The air whistled as he drew the rapier from its hilt.

"You must kill me before you touch my bride again!" Richard grimaced. He dodged side-to-side, slicing the night with his slender sword, while his left arm drew close to his

Circle of Love

body, hand pressed high against his chest.

Shaking the firearm in one hand, Dryden rushed the gangplank, while trying to draw a dagger with the other. Almost within range of Captain Allen's rapier tip, Dryden paused, cocked the pistol, and aimed again at Richard's moving figure.

Suddenly, Dryden's knee injury betrayed him. His weight shifted on the uneven wooden board beneath his feet. One ankle made a wrenching turn and gave a grossly unnatural twist to the leg. It pitched the man sideways. The pistol flew out of his grip, clattered on the walkway, and began to slide downward toward the dock. Dryden teetered a few seconds, clinging to the safety rope. Then he fell into the brackish waters below.

Richard leaped the final few feet to the ship and grasped Honour in his arms as if Dryden still tried to wrest her away. Then he abruptly released the fierce embrace and slumped against his wife, knocking her against the cabin of the ship.

"Richard!" Drunk with joy that he was alive, she held him hard. Then she drew back slightly and with her right hand caressed his face. His jaws were clenched, and his mouth made a straight line. Something sticky grazed her cheek. She raised her hand again and felt his blood in her hair. And saw the burn in the shoulder of his jerkin.

His voice sounded reedy. "Honour." Then his knees buckled.

Samuel rushed to help support Richard. "Let us take him below deck and clean the wound. And find out if the bullet lodged, or—please, God!—passed cleanly through."

Richard struggled to lift his head. He took a final glance at the dark water. Dryden had disappeared. He looked into Honour's face. She was safe, but at the high price of a human life.

The Cavalier remembered his prayers for protection. As he fought to stay conscious, he spoke in a thin voice, "*'Thou preparest a table before me, in the presence of mine enemies...'"*

* * *

As the *Sunrise* slipped from its mooring toward the dark Atlantic, three passengers carried Richard to the Sneade cabin. Young William separated his father's medical bag from the other trunks, then joined his mother and the others outside the door.

Samuel and Honour removed Richard's jerkin and inspected the wound. Nearly limp, he groaned and tried to reach around with his right hand. "My—back. The—back—of—my shoulder—throbs."

His eyes were sunken, half-closed in pain.

Samuel gently lifted Richard's left shoulder off the bunk in the dim cabin and probed awhile. The patient groaned again, barely swept along in waves of consciousness.

The physician straightened and looked Honour in the eye. "The bullet traveled through, thank God, for here's the hole it made departing." He stuffed a cloth tightly against it and reached for the disinfectant. "We will clean it after we finish the entry wound."

Honour nodded in agreement. She ran her hand across her husband's bare chest and felt his tremors of suffering. *The pain he endures for my sake!* Tenderly, following the shape of his collarbone, she continued to stroke him. As her touch neared his shoulder, she gasped. "Why, this bone is shattered!"

Richard winced and tried feebly to raise his good arm.

Honour bit her lip to hold back the tears. "Shhh, my love. You must be still."

"It is best to finish cleaning both wounds. Then we shall bind the shoulder lightly so he cannot move it. That is all we can do," said Samuel. "Pray there is no infection and let time be our healer."

Richard struggled to speak. "Sir—I already owe you—much."

"You are young and strong. I am doing the best for you I know how, and pray you will be well long before we land on the colonial shore." He tipped his head toward Honour. "'Tis in both our interests to do you good, eh?"

Samuel left the cabin for more supplies. Honour leaned over her husband and placed a gentle kiss on his trembling lips. "You offered up your life for me. How could I have ever trembled before you?" She gestured toward his torn flesh. "My enemy is dead because of your sacrifice. But now you must live so—so I can be a proper wife to you." A brief curve played on her lips, and Richard managed a wan smile. Then Honour slid to her knees beside his bunk to plead Richard's cause before their God.

Chapter Twenty

A fortnight later, the *Sunrise* still tacked back and forth toward the distant Virginia shore. It was early evening, and Richard stood with Honour on the deck of the ship. She wrapped her shawl tighter against the moist air. Richard carefully lifted his injured shoulder and encircled her waist with his left arm. She stood close to him for a long time, snugly held against his chest.

Before the sun disappeared below the wavy horizon, rays of light pierced the clouds and color played on the distant sea. Richard shifted against the rail, turning Honour's face toward his. Gentle lips teased hers like an inviting breeze. She read a question in his eyes. As if in answer, she reached up to stroke his pointed beard, then sealed her lips to his.

Delicious warmth and yearning for oneness spread through them both. Richard released her just long enough to regather her into a harder embrace. He spoke against her hair. "Honour, you are exquisite. *'Who can find a virtuous woman? for her price is far above rubies.'*" His words were jagged with emotion. "A gift from God, you are."

"As you are to me." She turned to face him with a

knowing smile. "My darling husband, the dark is falling quickly this night. We should go below."

They turned together and descended to their tiny cabin.

The God who created male and female surely smiled as the man and his wife, at last, gave themselves fully to one another.

* * *

Honour awakened first. She stretched lazily, recalling as in a haze, only half aware of all that had transpired. When her bare skin grazed Richard's broad back, she blushed, remembering it all. In spite of the morning chill, she grew suddenly warm. *So this is how it feels to be his wife.* She smiled at the memory of the union with the man she loved.

Richard stirred and rolled over. His arm lay across her. Silently, she thanked God for restoring his life to her.

Honour's eyes studied the face of her beloved—the youthful face beneath his shaggy mustache and beard. Viking blue eyes opened and he sat up, reaching to caress a strand of her dark hair.

"You are mine, truly mine. A blessing of beauty worth waiting for." He spoke softly, as if in awe.

Lifting Honour's hand to his lips, he kissed it. Then he stroked her ringless finger and frowned. "Oh, my love, forgive my haste from the barn the night of our marriage. The loss of your ring, and the license, plagues me so."

"Terror came swiftly. We were forced to fly. You cannot do it over again." Her voice was full of understanding.

"When my indenture is fulfilled, I promise you a ring, like unto the first. Surely a craftsman in the settlement can fashion another circle of love for the joy of my life."

Honour smiled at him in the morning light and touched his lips with her finger. "'Tis the man I desire, not the ring. But when someday you present the gift, I shall wear it until

Part II: Honour

death, a treasure of my heart. And instruct our children to pass it on to their children."

They spoke as one. "And their children's children."

Laughter welled up between them. When they grew quiet again, she molded herself against his body so he could cradle her. Husband and wife. Naked and not ashamed. They flooded together again like two streams rushing their banks, flowing as one vast river to the sea.

Part III: Anne

Chapter Twenty-one

Christopher stood beside Tracy Anne at the oriel window, almost afraid to touch her.

"I am not good for you. I must go," she repeated. Her words seemed so final.

A curtain of deep sadness wrapped around them both. His grief came as a crushing pressure in his chest. Hands uselessly at his sides, he stayed there, completely unaware of time.

Another tear slipped silently down Tracy's face. Her hand traveled to her throat and her body started to shake. "Chris—Christopher," she managed to whisper, "I think I'm dying." Her breathing came ragged and too fast, and her legs threatened to collapse underneath her.

Christopher pulled her into his chest, to keep her from falling. He could feel the rapid beating of her heart, the shallow breathing against his chest. "Stay with me, Anne, and don't pass out. I'm here with you, and I won't let you fall. Stay! We'll get through this together."

She wanted to interrupt her inward journey. But panic grabbed her again and imprisoned her in its grip. Her body temperature climbed, and she felt any moment she'd lose control completely.

But for the first time she felt she had an ally. It was almost as if fear and Christopher were waging the war, trying to pull her in opposite directions. Her body trembled against his, and he eased them both into the nearby chair. Settling her onto his lap, he began to rock her. "Oh, Anne, I love you so much. It grieves me to see you like this."

She took a ragged breath and looked away. "I—never—wanted you to know. I—tried to hide this—thing."

He took her face gently in one hand and turned it toward his, so he could look deeply into her dark eyes. "You probably did manage to hide it from everyone else. But I lived with you—remember?" He gave her an ironic smile. "And I saw you react to things, even when you didn't know I was paying attention."

She searched her pocket for a tissue and blew her nose. Then she stared out the diamond-shaped glass panes and twisted her hair around a finger. Where was that place of emotional safety she usually tried to imagine? It wasn't coming into focus in her imagination. Yet she felt some comfort right here, cradled on Christopher's lap.

"I saw, and I still love you." His voice was quiet. "I saw what happened a couple of times when you lost—something."

She looked up at him. "Or someone." A new tremor passed through her body.

He nodded. "Or someone..." *Like me?* he wondered.

* * *

Slowly, Christopher and Tracy Anne left the ancient house and walked toward her lodgings in the village. Her feet dragged along the gravel path.

"I don't want to lose you, too. But how can we start over with a fresh, new relationship, when I still battle this

Part III: Anne

monster?" She tried to let go of his hand, but he held on.

"Can't we work on it together?" He stopped under an aged yew tree and drew her down beside him on a bench.

She scanned the wide branches and her eyes widened. "This tree! This is the tree!" There was awe in her voice.

Christopher frowned at the sudden turn in her stream-of-consciousness. "I'm sorry, Anne. What about the tree?"

She took both his hands and turned her body to face him. "It's what I try to imagine when I'm afraid." Her eyes sparkled. "Someone told me once to think of something beautiful and safe when I feel the terror coming. And this looks just like 'my tree'!"

"I—I still don't understand. How can a tree—real or otherwise—help you feel better?"

"I'm not sure. But I think it has to do with how safe I felt with my grandparents, especially since my parents' relationship was such a mess." Tracy Anne paused, new understanding in her eyes. "There was a climbing cedar near the old farmhouse and I used to go there often. Its branches were so full near the top that I could hide and no one could see me. That's where I went after my father left—and—after Mother's—suicide."

"Oh, Anne. I never knew how she died."

"Everyone tried to tell me a blood vessel had burst in her brain. But I learned the truth later. She didn't die in her sleep; there were signs of an overdose in the teacup beside the bed."

"Was she so hurt by your father's unfaithfulness that she didn't want to live anymore?"

"Yeah. Even her daughter wasn't enough to make her want to live."

"How old were you, Anne?"

"Eight."

"So young to lose your parents."

"But old enough to know—too much—what was going

on." She shook her head. "I—I always wish I could redo that last night. You see, her death was really my fault."

Christopher shook his head. "How could you think that?"

"She had gotten to where she didn't care about anything. She'd quit crying and kind of shriveled up inside. Then one night she reached out and asked me if I'd sleep in her room, to keep her company. Independent prissy that I was, I refused." Tracy paused and swallowed. "Grampy and I found her the next morning." Tracy Anne's eyes had a haunted look, as she struggled not to cry.

Christopher put his arms gently around her and pulled her so close she could feel his heart beating. "No child should carry a burden like that." He spoke gently. "No adult either."

Tracy remained silent for a long time. A breeze came across the park and ruffled the green canopy stretched above them. "I—I think that's part of the reason I have these fears. When separation comes from the familiar, or from someone I—love..." She looked at Christopher. Her face exposed the depth of her feelings for him. "It doesn't even have to actually happen. I just think about it and lose control—no matter how hard I try not to!"

"Anne, I didn't study much psychology, but I think you've hit on something important. Having an idea of what starts the fears raging—well, maybe that's also the clue for getting them to stop."

Tracy Anne straightened. "Really? Do you think there's actually hope for getting over this?" She lowered her voice. "It's getting worse all the time. In childhood, there were a few times—like when my grandparents died, and I moved or changed schools. It even happened a few times living with you. After that, they've come more often—and a lot stronger, too. I'm not sure there's anything that can fix it."

"Oh, Anne, there's bound to be an answer. God doesn't

Part III: Anne

intend for you to be a prisoner to this. He wants you to be free from fear." Christopher's voice was earnest. "I've known a lot of people who needed a little help at some time in their lives, and therapy has made a big difference. Even in my own family."

"But I've already tried somebody my doctor recommended. We didn't get much of anywhere. He put me on some heavy-duty tranquilizers. I worried about getting addicted, so I stopped the pills—well, I stopped taking them regularly. I do keep a few for emergencies."

"Like what happened today?"

"Yeah. And I quit the sessions, too. He kept telling me to relax, but when I get like this my whole body screams, 'I can't!'"

"Maybe there's another way to approach it. I mean, you have one of the most creative minds I've ever worked with. You're in the perfect field for your abilities. The sky's the limit on your imagination and ideas..."

"That's just the trouble. When certain situations hit, I start to feel all these horrible things happening. And they are so real—and so awful!"

Christopher reached up to caress the pain in her face.

"Yes, they are. And we need to find someone who can help you defeat this..."

"Monster." She tossed her head. "It's taking over my life."

"Well, I'm no St. George, but I hereby commit myself to help you slay that dragon!" He smiled and took her hand playfully. And laid it over his heart. "Let's become co-conspirators and find a therapist to hunt down the monster and run a sword through its heart!"

"Christopher, now you're the weird one!" But she was smiling, and there was a saucy look on her face he hadn't seen in ages.

"Okay. Okay." He spread out his hands and looked up at

the branches above them. "I think maybe this is your tree."

She followed his gaze upward, then flashed him a teasing look. "Mmmmm. I dunno. The shape's a little off."

"Details, details! The main thing is, we dragon-slayers have got to stick together." He watched her reaction. "This means you can't go home—uh—yet."

Tracy Anne looked down and picked a long time at a hangnail. Then she slowly raised her head. "You win." The ghost of a smile played on her lips.

It's not everything, Christopher thought, *but it's a start.*

Chapter Twenty-two

The next morning Christopher caught up with Professor Leatherwood in the Senior Common Room, the old drawing room of the manor house. They seated themselves in overstuffed chairs, with a worn end table between them. A middle-aged lady appeared from the kitchen with a pot of tea. The young American poured them each a cup and added milk and a taste of sugar.

Christopher took a sip after stirring it. He still winced a little over the milk but was getting used to it, especially when there wasn't any fresh lemon around.

"Professor Leatherwood, I need a piece of advice. I know psychology's not your specific field, but you know your way around the University and the broader academic world. Do you know of anyone doing work on phobias, fears, anxiety and that sort of stuff?"

The archaeology scholar removed his half-glasses and patted his rumpled jacket. "Let me see." When he took a drink of the hot liquid, his heavy eyebrows wiggled. "I have a colleague—we were at Oxford together—who received his doctorate in psychology from a school in the States. Seems it was Southern California. He was working on a dissertation about—what exactly did he say?—yes, anxiety disorders, that's it. We haven't corresponded in some months, but I believe he's back in Britain, somewhere. Shall I look him up for you?"

Eagerness showed all over Christopher's face. "Oh, yes, sir. That would be such a help!"

"You're doing some kind of video project on the subject?"

Christopher shook his head. "No, it's for a friend. I'm looking for a therapist with experience in that area."

"Ah." The professor's brown eyes softened. "It wouldn't be for a certain brunette young lady, would it?"

"Yes, sir, it would."

"You have striking taste, my boy."

"Thank you, sir. When's a good time to come by your office?"

Leatherwood straightened his necktie. "What's today?"

"Tuesday."

He pulled up the tweed sleeve to glance at his watch. "Four o'clock will be fine."

"Thank you. I'll be there."

Professor Leatherwood stood and went out the tall carved doors.

Christopher gathered up his teaching materials for the next class. *This expert sounds good. I hope he's somewhere nearby.*

* * *

"York! Where's that?" Tracy Anne's voice level was increasing. Her conversation with Christopher threatened to carry to the next row of tables in the university dining room.

"Anne, it's not really that far. It's an easy drive up, or there's always the train. Only a couple of hours or so."

"I just get talked into staying awhile longer, and then I

Part III: Anne

get shipped off somewhere else I've never been before! And I'm not about to rent a car and go off on these roundabouts and carriageways, driving on the wrong side of the road!"

"Come on, Anne. All I've done for the last two days is ask around and call up people on the phone. Dr. Springer is the only therapist I could find anywhere around who knows about your kind of thing. I can't help it if he's up in York."

"Well, is my knight in shining armor coming with me?"

"To inspect Dr. Springer—or to slay a dragon?"

She sighed. "Both."

"Sure. Maybe we could get an appointment next Thursday afternoon, since I don't have any classes to cover after eleven."

"Okay." She used her business-negotiation voice. "If you'll come with me, I'll go."

"Deal. Let's go call the office now."

* * *

The following Thursday afternoon, Christopher and Tracy Anne stepped off the Inter-City to the hiss of hydraulics and the roar of wheels. Within just a few minutes, several other trains came and went through the huge shed-like structure of York station.

Tracy pointed to a yellow and blue engine of aerodynamic design, just pulling in on the track next to theirs. "What's that one?"

"It must be the fast train from London. I hear it reaches speeds of 125 miles per hour and can go from London to Edinburgh in just over four hours. York is the midway stop. Before my time at the university ends, I'd like to make that trip."

"Sounds interesting. Now, what do you know about finding Dr. Springer's office?"

"I have the address. Let's go on out and grab a taxi."

As they exited the station, Tracy looked across the city and pointed. "What's that giant church?"

"I'm sure it's York Minster. Professor Leatherwood said the cathedral towers over the whole city, that people get their bearings by looking for 'the Minster,' as they call it. If we have enough time, I'd like to go over and see it."

"Okay, but let's find the psychologist first." She looked up at him impishly. "And if that doesn't work, then we might try the church."

"Aw, Anne, you sound like such a cynic. It's a good thing I know there's a soft heart in there, too!" He raised his arm. "Taxi!"

As she stepped into the roomy black cab and placed her purse on her lap, Tracy murmured, "I hope this Springer fellow knows what to do."

* * *

The taxi driver lifted his plaid cap and turned to speak to his passengers. "We're nearly to tha address you give me." Then he pointed ahead. "There ya have it. Bootham Bar. One of the gates in the ancient Roman wall around the city, don't you know it. And, yonder, of course, that's the Minster."

Tracy Anne strained to understand the heavy Yorkshire dialect, while she absorbed the sights outside the cab window.

The car stopped on St. Mary's, just a few blocks away, in front of a townhouse with lace curtains in the front bay window.

Christopher paid, stepped out of the taxi, and held the door for Tracy Anne. He glanced down at the pocket calendar in his hand, then at two modest signs, side by side. "Springer Psychological Services" and "Tree Tops Guest House." His smile was full of confidence.

Part III: Anne

She leaned a moment on the iron fence. "It looks a lot more like a bed-and-breakfast than an office." Doubt produced tiny lines between her brows.

"Maybe the homey atmosphere is just what you need." He nudged her elbow and they climbed the steps together. She licked her lips, lifted the brass knocker, and waited.

Nothing could have prepared her for seeing the young woman who opened the varnished door. Tracy Anne's jaw dropped, and she could only stare.

"Tracy!" The tall, slender redhead threw her arms out wide and pulled the visitor into a bear hug.

Tracy finally found her voice. "Meg Bransford! What are you doing here, of all places?"

"Well, I'd like to know the same about you!"

Christopher just stood there with puzzlement on his face.

"Excuse my manners." Tracy hooked her arm through his. "Meg, this is Christopher Montgomery." She gestured toward her friend. "Meg Bransford. We were freshman suitemates at college. I can't believe you're here!"

Meg smiled and her green eyes glowed. "You, either! When I saw the new name in Dr. Springer's appointment book, I never dreamed it was really you." She motioned for them to come in the door and led them to a small parlor. "I just thought somebody here had the same name. What are you doing in England, anyway?"

"It's a long story, Meg, especially what brought me to see Dr. Springer. Christopher's teaching this semester at Keele in Staffordshire, and I came to visit. Then some things I've struggled with a long time came to a head, and a professor there thought Dr. Springer could help. So, here I am." She swallowed. "How in the world did you end up here?"

Meg invited them to be seated on a Victorian settee. She chose a rocking chair nearby. "After I transferred to USC, I changed my major to psychology, and eventually landed a counseling practicum here with Dr. Springer as my mentor. As soon as the internship is over, I'll have my Master's." The chair creaked.

"It seems like such a long time since we wore those silly beanies and struggled through freshman English. I was sorry we lost touch."

Meg crossed her legs and leaned toward Tracy Anne. "Me, too, Tracy."

"I'm not sure I ever told you how much it meant to have your friendship that first year away at school. Just having you there helped me get through a terrible time."

Meg smiled warmly. "I'm glad it did. Sometimes I wondered how you kept going, with school and work and not much family to help you out. No matter what happened, you always seemed to have the world by the tail."

"Apparently, it's got me now." Tracy sighed. "I'm having a lot of trouble with anxiety. Christopher tells me they call it a panic disorder."

"Well, you've come to the right place." Meg's attention shifted from her friend, as a door opened across the hall. "Here's Dr. Springer now."

A short, trim man emerged. His hair was gray, curling white at the temples. His eyes were clear, his voice kind. "Norman Springer." As the couple stood, he shook hands with each one. "And you must be Tracy Anne and Christopher." There was something unusual about the way he pronounced his words.

"I'm very happy you could see Anne, sir." Christopher's grip conveyed the sincerity of his words.

"And..." Tracy looked down and then met Dr. Springer's gaze. "I guess I'm glad to be here."

The therapist let out a soft laugh and touched his hand to her shoulder. "Getting started is the important thing. You're taking the right step."

Meg explained the newfound friendship with Tracy, and

Part III: Anne

the four of them visited a few moments.

As Dr. Springer and Tracy turned to go into the office, Christopher said, "Excuse me, sir, but I'm curious. Did you grow up here in Yorkshire?"

"As a matter of fact, I didn't." He grinned. "My brand of English comes from Nigeria. My parents were career missionaries there."

As Christopher sat down to wait, he thanked God for leading them to these people, in this place.

Chapter Twenty-three

Tracy Anne spent an hour in Dr. Springer's airy office. He asked questions and she answered, shyly at first but eventually won over by his skill and caring. He listened carefully. They even laughed together.

And Tracy cried. "Can I even get better? Just talking about my feelings makes me start shaking all over."

He picked up a box of tissues and handed it to her. "There's a lot we can do to help. Your difficulty has very specific known treatment. Treatment that works. We need to help you relax, change these destructive thought patterns, and deal with the separations that have happened in your life."

Tracy listened intently. "That's quite a bit to work on."

"Even something as simple as reducing your caffeine intake can help an anxiety-related condition." He paused and smiled. "Let me mention, too, that I pray for my clients. I see Jesus as a very active 'partner' in the healing process."

Dr. Springer looked at her kindly. "I also team with a psychiatrist, to check out possible physical causes and decide any medication you may need temporarily."

"I hope I won't need any." Tracy sniffed and clutched a tissue. "Back home, I tried that."

Circle of Love

"Well, it's different with each person. We'll discuss every step along the way carefully, and give you full information if you do need one of the anti-depressant or anti-anxiety drugs." He paused and touched his hands together at the fingertips. "Let's see now. I'm still confused on one important thing, up front. What are your immediate plans?"

"I don't even know how long I'm staying in England. Things are pretty mixed up right now."

"Well, we can make some steady progress if you take the train over once a week for several months, but we could accomplish much more if we had three sessions per week. That, though, would mean your staying in York for awhile."

Tracy sat, thinking. "I could ask Meg about staying on a couple of weeks with her."

"I can't speak for her, of course." The therapist's eyes twinkled. "But I'd be surprised if Margaret didn't make the most of this opportunity for the two of you to get reacquainted."

* * *

Christopher stood when Tracy Anne emerged from Dr. Springer's office. He stretched out a hand toward her. "Well, how did it go?"

She gestured toward the psychologist just entering the hallway. "I'd say he's joined the dragon-slayer team."

"Great." Christopher's eyes crinkled as he smiled. He lowered his voice to a conspiratorial whisper. "So, what's the strategy, Anne?"

"That's just what I want to talk over with you—and Meg, too." She glanced at her college friend, who'd been visiting with Chris between phone calls the last hour.

Meg placed a gentle hand on Tracy's arm. "Christopher tells me you're going back to Keele this evening. But I'd love to have more time with you." She smiled. "We have a

Part III: Anne

lot of catching up to do!"

Tracy Anne turned questioning eyes toward her boyfriend. "I—I would like to stay in York awhile, Christopher. Would you mind going back to the university without me? Dr. Springer says we can make better progress if we meet more than once a week."

"And I was about to invite you to stay over and see the sights of York with me—whether it's just overnight or for a week or two." Meg's mind whirred with plans already. "You see, Mrs. Springer operates Tree Tops, and I have the prettiest room in the whole guest house! There's a fabulous old wardrobe, and the tea tray's set with Wedgwood..."

"Whoa! What will Mrs. Springer think of all this?"

Meg gave her friend a reassuring touch, as she glanced toward her employer. "I really don't think she'll mind..."

"She'll be delighted, but just the same, I'll run up and ask her." Dr. Springer was already on the stairs.

Tracy looked at her purse by the settee. "I didn't bring anything for staying overnight."

"That's okay." Meg nodded her auburn curls. "You can borrow some of my things, and tomorrow—there's this great store, the Edinburgh Woolen Mill, and..."

Christopher chuckled at Meg's enthusiasm. "Anne, I could get your things at Keele and send them on up to you."

Dr. Springer came down the stairs and spoke to Tracy. "Claire is happy to have you."

"Such service!" Christopher laughed. "Counseling, friendship, a place to stay, and a tour guide, too!" He leaned close to Tracy's ear. "But I'll miss you while you're away."

She spoke softly, just for him. "It's better than running back to the States. I'd like to try facing it head-on this time."

"I'm proud of you." His whisper kissed her earlobe.

The front bell rang. "Margaret, I'll greet this last client today. Why don't you take your friends across the street for a bar snack and then show them the Minster?" Dr. Springer already had his hand on the doorknob.

What's so special about the cathedral? Tracy wondered as she went down the steps.

* * *

Inside the cozy neighborhood pub, Tracy Anne gaped at the food set before her. "You call this a snack?" A steaming platter with shepherd's pie, two kinds of potatoes, broccoli, and parsleyed carrots rested on a thermal placemat.

Meg looked at her own identical plate and smiled. "I don't, but they do here in Yorkshire."

"I'm starved! Let's pray." Christopher bowed his head, and gave thanks, not only for the meal but for the hope in his heart.

* * *

Meg leaned back in the Windsor chair and downed her last sip of ginger beer. "So, Christopher, when's the last train back? Do you have time to walk over to the Minster with us?"

He looked at his watch. "I still have an hour and a half. Can we walk from here and still get to the station?"

"Sure. And on the way we'll pass the ruins of St. Mary's Abbey, where they perform medieval mystery plays every few years." Meg paused and glanced across the table. "Ready to go, Tracy?"

"Okay, let's see this church I've been hearing so much about. You all make it sound like a big deal."

* * *

When the three left the quaint pub, it was already dark outside. Street lamps gave a golden glow to the cobblestone

Part III: Anne

streets as the group made their way toward York Minster. The ruins of St. Mary's stood solemn and silent, a jagged silhouette against the city sky. A few more twists and turns brought Tracy, Christopher and Meg to Bootham Bar.

"This is one of the remaining gates of the medieval city," said Meg. "You can even walk up there along the wall, but I like the view of the Minster best from right here."

Christopher and Tracy looked past the Bar's cross-shaped arrow slits to the three imposing towers beyond. The ancient church stood out in brilliance from the night sky. And then its bells began to ring.

"If only I had the Betacam here!" Christopher said. His hands twitched as if to frame up the stunning video shot. "A roll-focus off the gate and chimney pots to the church would look great."

The bells sang their message through the clear, cool air. Tracy Anne stood still, just absorbing the sound. When she finally spoke, her voice was full of awe. "I want to memorize the bells' beauty. I'd give anything to take that home in my heart."

Christopher took her hand and gave it a squeeze. "Let's walk on over and go inside."

As they set foot in the cavernous stone church, a woman wearing a bulky sweater walked over to greet them. Her sensible shoes echoed in the vast space. "Tourists? Or are you here for Evensong?"

Meg's eyes formed a question, as she looked at her friends.

"It's a short service." The lady's voice welcomed without being pushy.

"Thank you," Tracy murmured, "but I think we'll just look around quietly."

The lady nodded. "If you have any questions, I shall be happy to help." Then she smiled pleasantly and left them.

Through an arched doorway came the strains of a hymn,

lending a reverent mood for viewing the craftsmanship of centuries. The three visitors continued down the main aisle toward the choir area. Magnificent wrought-iron gates, embossed in gold, stood alongside statues of English monarchs, while intricate wood carving richly decorated other portions of the church. The vaulted ceilings drew Christopher's eyes upward along the walls, past the heraldic shields all the way to the golden roof bosses.

Meg pointed high into the shadows. "These bosses look like small rosettes but they're actually three feet across. Each tells a story from the Bible. The stained glass, the bosses, even the cross shape of the building...everything was designed to picture the truth of the Gospel."

Tracy thoughtfully examined the work of dedicated hearts. "The original audio-visual for the unread masses."

"And embellished by generation after generation of common folk, wanting to honor God with their effort." Christopher shook his head. "And now everybody wants everything instantly, or even yesterday!"

And when we get it, we soon throw it away, Tracy thought. A narrow stairway near the vestry captured her attention. While Meg studied a piece of carving, Tracy led Christopher over to the side. "Why, look at these steps. The stone is actually worn down from all the priests." She knelt and touched the cool, smooth surface. "Just imagine how many have served here, all these hundreds of years."

Christopher spoke gently. "It took a lot of faithful believers, most whose names we've never heard, to keep the faith so it could be passed along to us." He looked intently at Tracy Anne, and drew her back to her feet. "What a tragedy it would be, after two thousand years, for our generation to drop the torch, to fail in passing it along."

"Christopher." Tracy's eyes widened. She still held onto his hands. "Now, I know what's happened to you. Why you're so different from before. You really believe this, and

Part III: Anne

you're trying to live it, aren't you?"

He nodded and let out his breath. "That's what it's all about, Anne. I didn't want to hit you over the head, but I recommitted my life to the Lord a few months ago. I just wanted you to see it's real, that Jesus is making a new person out of me."

"That's kind of scary, though. At least, I knew the other guy." She made an attempt to laugh, but it was hollow.

"Please don't let it spook you, Anne. The passion for you is still there, isn't it?" He gave her a message with his eyes, and squeezed her hands.

Suddenly it all made sense to Tracy. *That's why he's been driving me crazy! His feelings are powerful as ever, but since we're not married, he won't sleep with me.*

"Now I love you deeper, wider and, uh, regardless of your struggles. I'm trying to love you like God loves me, just as I am, unconditionally."

She was silent for a long time. "If He can love me like you do, that's the best news I've ever heard."

Without words, Christopher hugged her to himself.

* * *

Later that evening, after seeing Christopher to the train station, the two women returned to Tree Tops. Tracy sat down on the extra bed in Meg's room and ran her hand thoughtfully over the blue-sprigged down comforter, while her hostess plugged in the kettle and set up the tea tray.

Meg grinned as she reached for a carton of milk, keeping cool on the windowsill. "Almost as good as a refrigerator, this time of year." She banged the sash closed, adjusted the lace curtains, and poured Tracy Anne a cup of tea. "If you think the Minster's impressive after dark, just wait until you see the medieval glass in the daylight! The great east window is larger than a tennis court." She paused for a quick breath. "In fact, I hear it's the largest expanse of stained glass in all of England."

Tracy added a spoonful of sugar to the tea, only half listening. Her gaze kept straying to the Minster, visible through the curtains, as it towered over the city. At last, she spoke softly. "I'm going back tomorrow morning, to see the windows come alive."

And she did, alone. Kneeling in the chapel, facing the great window, she traced with her eyes the old stories her grandparents used to tell her. She pondered the change in Christopher's life. And as she looked at the apex of the east window, picturing God on His throne, she gave her failures to Him. In the filtered light of an English morning, far more than colored glass radiated life. Tracy Anne Stevens was reborn.

When the majestic bells of York Minister rang later in the day, Anne paused to listen. *Wherever I go from here, I'll take more than the beauty of the bells with me. And besides, I think I've already come home.*

Chapter Twenty-four

Christopher took the train from York to Stoke-on-Trent, with a lighter burden on his heart for Anne than he'd carried for a long time. When he stepped out of the taxi into the shadow of Keele Hall, he met Professor Leatherwood coming up the walkway.

"Christopher, my man." He shuffled a stack of books in his arms to clap the young man on the shoulder. "Gone just a day and you've missed all the excitement."

"Really? So what's going on?"

"This noon, I'm sure you're aware, was the groundbreaking for the new library." A book nearly slipped from his grasp. He caught it and rebalanced the pile.

"That's right. I missed it, taking Anne up to York."

The professor's eyes danced over his half-glasses. "You'll never guess what happened!"

Intrigued to see Leatherwood so enthused, Christopher smiled and willingly fell for the conversational bait. "Well, what?"

"There's been an historical discovery, square in the midst of the building site. You know, that wooded fern dell just across the lane from the existing library?"

Christopher nodded.

"And the vice-chancellor of the university has asked me to conduct the investigation."

"That's great. What did they find?"

"One of the first strokes of the ceremonial shovel, it was, too! It turned up a sealed crock—seventeenth century—with a metal object rattling around inside. I'm on my way to the lab, now." His body almost twitched with expectancy. "Nothing else lay around it, so it was carried over there this afternoon, fully intact. A team of us plan to open it straight away, this evening."

Christopher, reluctant to dampen his enthusiasm, nevertheless gave his friend a skeptical look. "How do you know it's that old? Maybe it's just a Victorian relic, or something left over from the troops stationed here in the 1940's?"

"Ah, but it cannot be. It bears marks and characteristics that belong only to Rhenish ware of, oh, about 1615 to 1660." The professor started walking again.

Christopher reversed his original direction and fell into step beside him. "What's Rhenish ware?"

"It's a particular, squat style of ceramic made in the Rhineland area."

"But isn't that—modern Germany? How would it be buried here?"

Leatherwood gestured toward the books under his arm. "I've already done some checking. Vessels such as this were in common usage among the English gentry during that period. Their sons were off fighting wars on the Continent, and commerce enterprises crossing the Channel were plentiful."

"What do you think's inside?"

They neared the steps of an academic building. The professor motioned with his head toward the entrance. "How about coming with me to find out?"

"All right, I will. Here, let me get the door." The young

Part III: Anne

lecturer went along for the fun, with no idea of the implications the discovery would bring.

* * *

When they entered the lab, two others waited beside a high table for Professor Leatherwood.

He set the books on a counter and clapped his hands briskly. "Christopher Montgomery, meet Graeme Smith. He also has studied the Mayfield family and our Hall as a hobby for twenty years."

Christopher extended his hand to Dr. Smith. "My mother is a Mayfield." He grinned. "American branch." He reached to shake hands with the graduate student beside them. "And John and I have already worked together. He's a terrific sketch artist."

"Good." Leatherwood nodded at the wooden crate on the table, then flipped on a bright light. He donned gloves and picked up a tool from the wide assortment already laid out. "Let's get started."

Carefully, the team of experts lifted the crock from the surrounding soil contained in the box. With several delicate chisels and brushes, they removed most of the clay from the exterior of the piece. John drew rapidly with his pencil and noted the professors' comments while they measured, explored and discussed. He also took photographs. Expectancy grew with each movement of the jar, as the objects inside shifted and teased the small group.

Professor Leatherwood related what he'd already learned. His fingers gingerly handled the ceramic, turning it this way and that, examining the bottom for any markings. "Here's where our groundbreaking spade chipped it." His finger settled into a recess. Dr. Smith sifted the earth and recovered the sliver.

Christopher knew he should stand back from the table,

Circle of Love

out of their way. His weight shifted from one foot to another, and he leaned against the wall. From there he glanced around the lab itself for the first time: a marked-up map of the Middle East on one wall, the untidy stacks of British Museum magazines, and general hodgepodge lying around in no apparent order. But each time the metal object clinked against the ceramic, it called him closer to their work area. Soon, he bent over the table beside the others.

Dr. Smith inspected the outside characteristics at length, and confirmed, "Definitely Rhenish ware, first half of the seventeenth century." His forehead was pink with enthusiasm against the thatch of white hair.

Leatherwood slowly circled the seal around the jar lid with his fingers. "It appears to be fully intact." To Christopher he added, "That increases the likelihood of the contents being well preserved."

He pried the waxy substance away from the rim, a piece at a time, and laid each bit on the piece of graph paper John provided.

At last, when Christopher despaired of ever seeing inside, Leatherwood lifted the cover and peered in. With a gentle tug, he released the meagre contents. They lay on the tabletop.

A small piece of parchment, tightly curled and broken around the edges.

And a circle of metal, tarnished dark. A ring.

Leatherwood motioned for Smith to take over. Christopher held his breath. John sketched furiously, then switched to the camera.

With infinite patience, the historian began to unroll the parchment. "The ink is quite faded." He drew the special light down close to the work area. "There's a date. The year of our Lord 1642." He paused while he unrolled a bit more. "Why, it appears to be a marriage license. Indeed, a special license."

Part III: Anne

Graeme Smith turned to Christopher. "Only an archbishop could issue such a license in those days."

All attention shifted back to Smith. "There's a seal and signature: William Cantuar, Cantuar being the abbreviation for Canterbury. By this, it appears Archbishop Laud signed the document. That's puzzling. I could swear he languished, all but forgotten, in the Tower of London during that period."

"And later, of course, was beheaded," said Leatherwood.

John stopped taking notes. "So, who are the lucky bride and groom?" Chuckles broke the tension in the room.

Professor Leatherwood leaned over Smith's shoulder. He pushed his glasses higher on his nose. "Can you make out the names?"

"It's—a Captain Richard—Allen, and an Honour—Mayfield." Suddenly, Smith became agitated. "Mayfield!" He put his hand to his forehead. "That's—that's quite possibly the daughter of Mayfield Manor who disappeared in the early months of the Civil War!"

Christopher's face paled. He looked in futility around the lab for a telephone. "What time is it in Texas? Where's the closest phone? I've got to call my mother!"

No one even answered him.

He flipped through his wallet for a calling card. "I have to call America, now! Where's the nearest phone?"

"Don't leave now. We haven't examined the ring yet." Professor Leatherwood tossed the words over his shoulder. He never even looked up.

Chris paused just inside the doorway.

John stopped working to ask, "Was the wedding performed? Does it say?"

"Yes. John Whitehead, the vicar, signed it on the 12th of November, 1642." Leatherwood pointed at the document.

An expression of sudden clarity crossed Dr. Smith's features. "Of course. She must have eloped with a soldier.

Circle of Love

Her mother never saw her after that night the Roundheads attacked and looted the Hall. And I seem to recall from military records that a Cavalier commander turned up missing about the same time."

"But where did they go?" John almost bounced like a child.

Smith frowned. "No one knows. Neither was ever heard of again, as far as the family records show. And the church register reports no marriage. I got curious and ran that down a couple of years ago myself. But I hit a dead end."

In the silence, Christopher's voice was low. "I have an idea they went to America."

Surprise registered on every face in the room.

"Why do you think so?" asked Smith.

Chris cleared his throat. "My mother and her sister Ruth are genealogy fanatics. Mom's gone over it with me a hundred times and dragged me to more reunions than I care to count." The rest of his response came out in a rush. "There's a database in Ohio with all the details, and even an American association of Mayfields. Mom descends from a Matthew Mayfield, born in 1643 in Henrico County, Virginia, the only live birth to a Richard Allen and Honour Mayfield." The young American paused. "You see, our family has enjoyed a fine Christian heritage. It's always been a—wart on the family pride that Matthew was, uh, an illegitimate child."

Leatherwood smiled and put a hand on Christopher's shoulder. "Perhaps he wasn't born on the wrong side of the blanket, after all, my boy."

"Well, what are you waiting for?" John set down his clipboard. "Run; don't walk! There's a phone under the stairway. Call your mom, now! It's just dinnertime in Texas anyway."

Leatherwood called after his young friend. "Don't you want to see the ring?" But Christopher was already halfway

Part III: Anne

down the hall.

* * *

The next morning, Christopher found the professor in the lab. Leatherwood was reviewing the events of the night before, as he looked over John's notes and sketches.

"Professor Leatherwood, let me tell you what I learned from the family back in Texas."

"And I have more to tell you about the ring. You ran off before you got a good look at it."

Christopher smiled. "I did, all right. But I found out some pretty intriguing stuff."

"Like what?"

"That Richard Allen and Honour Mayfield embarked at Southampton in November 1642 and arrived at Jamestown in December."

Leatherwood shivered. "A jolly Advent season that must have been on the North Atlantic."

"They traveled on the *Sunrise*, to be exact. And our family computer wizard in Ohio has a copy from the Virginia State Archives of a land grant naming them as servant and companion to Samuel and Alice Sneade."

The professor whistled. "Anything else?"

"Just that on the passenger list Honour signed her name as Honour Mayfield Allen."

"Well, well."

"Oh, and there's one more thing. I'm expecting some faxes this afternoon, one from Ohio of the land grant, and another after Mom goes to open her safe deposit box. There's a ring that's been handed down in the family that by tradition, at least, belonged to Matthew Mayfield's mother."

"Have you ever seen the ring?" Excitement sparked in the professor's eyes.

"Only once, as a teenager. Mom described it to me last

night. It's a silver band, about three-eighths of an inch wide. Once upon a time, there must have been some decoration, but it's nearly worn smooth now."

Leatherwood motioned Christopher over to the lab table, put on his gloves, and turned on the light. "Does this look anything like it to you?"

The American peered at it intently. Unlike the object that emerged from the crock last night, it shone argent bright. "You've polished it?"

"Yes, we worked on it late into the night. Had to be very careful."

"I can imagine."

"Say, Christopher, did your mother mention any kind of inscription inside the ring?"

He shook his head. "There's none that I know of, and the ring apparently was worn a lot before the family started pampering it."

"I just wondered. We found one—no, two—in the ring last night. And it seems to be in perfect condition, as if it's never been worn. It's not even scratched."

"What does the engraving say?" Eagerness rushed into Christopher's voice.

The professor almost seemed to be playing games with him. "Ring me when your faxes arrive this afternoon. Then I'll meet you down here, and we'll have a look together." He turned the circle of silver this way and that, with a smile of satisfaction on his face.

* * *

When the fax machine spit out its message, Christopher absorbed the historical contents with excitement. But the P.S. at the bottom rocked him. He just stared at it.

Didn't you work with a Drake Flint a few

years ago? I saw in the morning paper that he drove his BMW into a concrete barrier on the tollway late last night. The police said he was full of cocaine. So sad.

Anne will be relieved, in a way, but how awful for him.

For several minutes, Chris just sat, thinking. Finally, he reached for the phone. "Professor, the faxes are here."

"Right. I'll meet you downstairs."

Christopher and Leatherwood arrived about the same time. The archaeologist unlocked the lab and they went in.

"Let me see your faxes, while you read what's inside the ring. Then let's compare notes. Here, use these gloves." The professor scanned the documents from America. "Mmm. Hummm." Twice, he pushed his glasses back up on his nose.

Christopher held up the circle of love in his fingers. Each rosebud and ivy leaf stood out in bold relief around the band. The words "Thou and thou only" intertwined with the design. Then he peered closely at the engraving inside. "R.A. et H.M.," he whispered. But there was more. "Professor," he called out, "have you got a Bible in here somewhere?"

Leatherwood patted his shirt pocket. "Not on me, but there's one on the desk." He quirked an eyebrow. "In fact, there was a verse I needed to look up just last night."

"Oh, really. I'll bet it's the same one I want now—First John 4:19."

"Sure is." The professor moved a magazine that covered an open Bible. "The First Epistle of St. John, chapter 4, verse 19. 'We love him: because he first loved us.'"

Christopher was quiet for a moment, then he raced to where the faxes lay. "Listen to this!" He shuffled the pages. "Here it is. 'There appears to be an inscription on the inside of the ring. The central portion is more readable than the edges. We believe that part says 'Jn. 4.'" He looked up. "Whoa, man, this is amazing!"

"I thought so myself, when I read it a minute ago. Do you suppose the couple lost their license and ring, and Richard had another one made for her?"

Christopher nodded. *Wait until I tell Anne about this!*

Chapter Twenty-five

Back in Christopher's room, the phone rang before he even had time to get out his calling card. "Hello."

"Hi!"

"Gosh, Anne, this is incredible. I was just about to call you!"

"Well, something really amazing happened this morning, and I couldn't wait to share it with you!" There was a joy in her voice he'd never heard before. "I've been calling you all day."

"Some pretty interesting events have gone on here, too, since yesterday. They've kept me running around all day long. But what's up with you? You sound so happy!"

"I am. Oh, Christopher, I am. It was great enough to meet Dr. Springer yesterday and feel hope. I mean, we're going to defeat this panic. I just know it."

"That's fantastic! But there's more?"

"Right. And it's even more important than that. I, uh, I was sitting in the Minster this morning and I—well, I told God I've loused up my life pretty good. And I asked Him to forgive me and make my life brand new." Her voice was husky with emotion. "And I just know He'll help me with my fears, too. He already has!"

"Oh, Anne. That's the most wonderful news you could ever give me. I'm so glad!" His heart raced with joy.

"I thought you'd feel that way."

"When can I see you? I'm stuck directing a student production tomorrow all day, but after that—or on second thought, maybe I can get it covered..."

"Don't do that, Christopher. I'm dying to see you, too, but I think I need another session or two under my belt—to deal with this new development. Just another two or three days here, then I'll return to Keele. We could spend a few days together. After that, I need to come on back to York for a week."

"Well, if that's what you want to do..."

She gave a big sigh. "It's not what I want to do, Christopher. It's what I feel I must do."

He nodded, although she couldn't see him. "I understand the difference. Just call me so I can meet you at the station."

"You bet I will. And—you said something's going on there. What's happening?"

He argued with himself for a moment. *Should I tell her now, or show her in person?* "You know, I think we're in for even more new developments. I'd like to let you in on the whole surprise when you get here." He paused. "There is some news from home I need to tell you now."

"It's not good, is it? I can tell."

"Well, you're right, in a way. Um, I just heard from Mom, and she saw a news piece on Drake."

"They arrested him robbing a bank." Her voice was filled with sarcasm.

"No, Anne. He's dead. A car wreck while he was high on cocaine."

There was silence on the line. She just listened numbly. "So—so my nightmares can't come true now, can they,

Part III: Anne

Chris?"

"Nope. But his worst ones have just begun."

She exhaled a big breath into the phone. "I'm relieved, but, oh, for him....Was anybody else hurt?"

"I don't know." He straightened his shoulders. "Look, there's a great find for you to look forward to when you get here. Let's concentrate on that, okay?"

"It'll be hard to wait. You've got my curiosity going."

"It'll be worth it, Anne, I promise."

"Christopher, I trust you." Her voice grew soft. "And—I love you."

Three little words. Three words of commitment she'd always seemed unable to say. He pressed a fist against the hammering in his chest. "Oh, Anne, I love you." *I've always loved you.*

She whispered, "See you in a few days," and there was a gentle click.

The longest few days of my life. Christopher's head spun with possibilities for the future, while his heart felt like dancing.

* * *

The morning of Tracy Anne's arrival, Christopher waited in the front room of his lodgings and listened for a delivery van. Shortly before eleven, an overnight express truck drew up outside, and Christopher rushed through the door and down the steps. He signed to confirm receipt of the heavily insured red, white and blue box, and then hurried to his room.

After opening the medium-sized parcel and separating out the padding material, he unwrapped the small object and laid it in the palm of his hand. He turned it this way and that, held it up to the light, and felt the slight texture of its metallic surface.

Then he dialed Professor Leatherwood's office phone. "It's here! I'd like to bring it over."

"That's splendid! My morning classes are over, and I've just returned from another search in the archives with Graeme."

"Really? Did you find what you were looking for?"

"I believe there's a scrap of a certain young lady's journal you'd be interested to see. It's damaged and incomplete, but the few pages that survive begin in September 1642."

By the time the professor laid down the receiver, Christopher had already grabbed his jacket and slammed the door.

* * *

Christopher stood on the station platform and glanced at the big clock face. It was 4:57 pm. The train was already two minutes late. He took off his glasses and placed them in the vest pocket of his jacket. For the umpteenth time that afternoon, he felt for the small lump buttoned into his shirt pocket. It was still there.

A cold draught ruffled his light hair. The weather was so like that day not long ago when Tracy Anne first arrived.

But for Christopher, and Anne, nearly everything had changed.

A blue engine lumbered past, then a passenger car and another. Christopher scanned the windows for a familiar face. At the end of the fifth car, he saw her, half-standing, her face pressed to the window. She was laughing.

He threw her a kiss and ran toward the train door. She handed a beat-up suitcase down the steps to him, and Christopher plopped it on the ground. Then he reached out his arms, and Anne filled them.

She felt firm and snug against his body, while he ran his hands up and down her back, caressing her heavy hair. After

Part III: Anne

feasting on her closeness, he loosened the embrace and tipped her face to his. Her lips reached for his swiftly, with a hunger and sureness beyond any memory they'd shared. Her familiar taste and scent enveloped him completely.

At last, Anne leaned back slightly to see his face. "Christopher." Her voice was round with joy. Her eyes, so alive.

"Welcome home, Anne." His eyes spoke volumes more.

She went up on tiptoe to kiss a laugh line beside his left eye.

"I'll have to leave my glasses off more, if this is the kind of greeting I get." He swung one arm around her waist and picked up the baggage with the other.

She leaned close against his shoulder as they walked from the station toward the bus stop. "Christopher, I'm so glad you took me to York. In just a few days the whole world seems different. Meg has been such a help, and Dr. Springer..." She drew a quick breath and plunged on. "Why, he understands what's going on with me and says lots of other people have struggles like mine. I'm not alone in it. And he knows what to do to help me through it, to change the way I talk to myself."

She paused long enough to miss an uneven place in the walkway. "And that cathedral! No wonder everybody says you have to go to there several times to take it all in. Down deep in that undercroft, Christopher," she tugged at his sleeve, "did you know it's got layers and layers of history on top of each other? There's the old Norman church ruins— you can tell by the rounded arches—then they built the medieval cathedral on it. That part has the pointed windows. And right nearby, there's all kinds of Roman garrison stuff, and you've just got to see the Viking Museum. Imagine, those houses, tools, and even shoes preserved for years in a peat bog!"

Christopher stopped at the corner, put down the suitcase,

and faced Anne. "Whoa, there!" He placed his arms on her shoulders and gave her a big grin. "I can tell you're just a bit excited about all you've been doing."

She gave him a sheepish smile. "What an awful chatterbox, Christopher. I'm sorry."

"That's okay." He gave her a quick hug. "I happen to love a certain chatterbox and want to hear all about it. How about slowing down just a leetle bit so I can digest it all!"

"I just realized something." She looked down briefly. "You have news, too, and I haven't even asked you about it."

He gave her a reassuring look. "How about a leisurely dinner in our favorite old inn, and I'll tell you the whole story." He squinted and touched his shirt pocket lightly.

"That sounds wonderful."

A red bus rumbled up in a swirl of diesel fumes, and the couple got on. They climbed the steps to the second level and settled into place.

Tracy Anne reached for Christopher's hand. "Now, would you like to know what happened to me in the church that morning?"

* * *

The coals glowed orange in the grate of the Black Horse Inn. Since it was much too early for the dinner crowd, the couple had the low-beamed room to themselves. Christopher seated Anne at an intimate table in the corner near the fire. Its warmth and cheer reflected in her eyes.

Christopher relaxed in the high-backed bench opposite her. He studied her quietly, as she picked up the menu. *You are like a new person*, he thought. "Anne, a woman of faithfulness and loyalty graced by God. How you fit your name tonight," he murmured.

She gave him a quizzical look, then smiled. "Is that why you've always called me by my middle name?"

Part III: Anne

"Partly." He took her hand in his. "When I first met you, I just liked 'Anne' better for you. Behind all that business, I felt a sensitive heart. And the way the Lord's been working in your life, I prefer it even more." He caressed her hand with his thumb, and looked into her eyes. A thought struck him and his mustache twitched. "But if you were Clementine Bushwhacker, I couldn't love you more than I do right now."

Anne laughed freely, and Christopher joined in.

Then she grew serious and stretched out her hand to touch his face. "Christopher." She savored his name before she went on. "A long time ago, a wonderful man invited me to commit my life to his. At the time, I felt pressured, scared. I couldn't make a decision like that. I was too bound up in my fears and hurts." She swallowed and grasped his hand for courage. "Now I know how much I hurt him. But I think I'm starting to learn what real love is. Love that cares no matter what." Her voice grew shaky. "Do you think he'd ever risk asking again?"

Lines of joy sprang to the corners of Christopher's eyes. He slid off the opposite seat and onto the bench where Anne waited. Her heart leaped when he gathered her into his arms and placed a passionate kiss on her lips, then on her throat, and lingered in that sensitive spot below her earlobe. She returned his affection with a warmth to match.

Slowly, he eased back enough to see her face. "Anne, my love, will you be my wife—forever?" His lips were parted, eager for her answer.

"You know I will." Her eyes glowed, and her voice sounded breathless. "Oh, yes, Christopher! Yes!"

He reached over and brushed away a single tear that clung to her lashes. Then his arms encircled her as if they wouldn't let go for centuries.

* * *

Later, Christopher unbuttoned his shirt pocket and removed a tiny object wrapped in silvercloth. "Anne, what would you think of this as a wedding ring?"

In his palm lay a gleaming circle of silver. He turned it slowly to reveal the patina of age and vague inscription it bore. "Before you answer, may I tell you a story?"

She nodded, intrigued.

He lifted up the delicate ring in his fingers. "It's quite a long tale."

Anne shifted slightly, gave his leg a gentle touch, and smiled. "I have all the time in the world."

Epilogue

*H*er face radiant, Anne snuggled closer to Christopher's side as he led her outside through the old oak door. After clearing her heavy brocade skirt, he fumbled with the ancient hardware and shut the dark chill of the candlelit church behind them.

The wheezing melody of "Ode to Joy" faded as the door swung closed.

A sudden rush of sunlight caught the golden threads of Anne's ivory gown. Each strand seemed to reflect the brightness.

Chris turned to face his bride. Gently, he touched the wreath of flowers encircling her head and felt her luxuriant hair. Then he tilted her face to his for a lingering kiss. "Happy?" he whispered at last.

Anne reached up an elegant sleeve and ran her hand down her beloved's chest, tapping every ruby stud on his tuxedo shirt. She flashed him an impish smile and gave his tapestry cummerbund a snap with her fingernail. "Awash in a river of happiness..."

A grin broke out across his face.

Her heart swelled beneath the square-necked bodice. She looked down at the heirloom on her left hand. Honour's ring. Now, her own wedding ring. A priceless circle of love. Unending. Unbroken. "Oh, Christopher! Never, never did I think we'd be doing this!"

Christopher lifted her small hand and gazed at her. Their eyes communicated their hearts. "You are worth the wait, Mrs. Montgomery."

"I hope so, Chris." Her voice sounded unsteady. The fragrant blooms in her right hand trembled.

A spring breeze rustled the ribbons flowing from her bouquet. Rich burgundy, blue and gold streamers fluttered across the dress patterned after a seventeenth-century gown.

"You remind me of a Maypole, all wrapped in color."

Anne lowered her lashes almost shyly. "Right now I feel more like a virgin bride."

Christopher's chest tightened with emotion. "Before God—and me—you are. With him, we have made a new beginning."

He looked from his wife toward the stone steeple. "I thought this day would never come." As if on cue, the bells began to ring.

Their cascade of joy filled the air on the Staffordshire hilltop. And even the daffodil trumpets danced as the April breeze swept Anne and Christopher into another tender embrace.

About the Author

Susan Cornell Bauer co-founded Alpha Video Productions with her husband Gary in 1981. She currently serves as writer/producer and administrator.

Circle of Love is her first novel. Susan has enjoyed writing since high school. Her projects include scripts, articles, newsletters, press releases, family history, editing books and manuals for non-profit organizations, and some poetry and drama. Video productions have taken her to England, Guatemala, Honduras, Mexico, Portugal, Ukraine (former Soviet Union), as well as various locations in the continental U.S., Alaska, and Hawaii.

She is a *summa cum laude* graduate of Belhaven College, Jackson, Mississippi, where she met her husband. The Bauers have two adult daughters, Sara and Claire, and live in the Dallas area.

Susan is a recipient of World Vision's Award of Excellence and, with her husband, was named 1999 Alumni of the Year by Belhaven College. Awards for their joint video productions include the New York International Film Festival, Telly Award, Videographer Award, and Communicator Award.

Personal hobbies include reading, music listening, travel, and history. Susan and Gary are active members of Lake Ridge Bible Church in Mesquite, Texas.

A Personal Word to the Reader

Thank you for taking time out of your busy life to read this story! While it should not be considered autobiographical, I don't mind sharing with you that I have struggled since childhood with irrational fears and anxiety. Some of the very things that helped Tracy Anne have allowed me to deal with worry and panic.

Because of my personal relationship with Jesus Christ and the peace He gives, I enjoy a fulfilling life, complete with travel to faraway places like Eastern and Western Europe, Central America, and Mexico, rather than existing in an ever-shrinking world of my own home or bedroom. God's freedom is a wonderful gift! The credit belongs to Him!

Some Bible references that have been a great encouragement to me include:

Jeremiah 29:11-13   (God's plans for good, to give hope and a future)
Lamentations 3:19-26   (God's daily faithfulness)
Matthew 6:25-34 and 7:7-11   (Jesus' teaching on worry and seeking God)
I Peter 5:7   (letting God carry our anxiety)
Philippians 4:6-8   (the peace of God and positive focus of our minds)
Hebrews 13:5b-6   (God's promise never to leave us)

Reading the Bible and praying are powerful antidotes to worry and anxiety.

For more understanding of anxiety and practical steps in dealing with it, I recommend Dr. Archibald D. Hart's book, *The Anxiety Cure: You Can Find Emotional Tranquillity and Wholeness* (Nashville: Word Publishing, 1999, ISBN 0 8499 1532 5). Visit www.archibaldhart.com for a complete list of his books.

To find out how you can make a new beginning through a personal relationship with Jesus Christ, call the toll-free number below. Caring people are available to guide you in the most important life decision you'll ever make.

1-888-NEED-HIM

There's also information on the Alpha Video website to assist you. Visit www.alphavideo.net and click on "How to," then "How to live forever."

I heard about the concept of "secondary virginity" through Focus on the Family. It seems to me a beautiful example of God's grace and wise behavioral change for those seeking a fresh start sexually. Contact them by mail at Focus on the Family, Colorado Springs, Colorado 80995, call them at 1-800-A-FAMILY, or visit their website at www.family.org. Most of the materials on this subject are aimed at teens but contain principles valid for any age group.

If you enjoyed *Circle of Love* and/or found it helpful, I would love to hear from you. *Soli Deo Gloria.*

Affectionately,

Susan Cornell Bauer
alphagb@aol.com
Alpha Video Productions
1219 Abrams Road, Suite 316
Richardson TX 75081 USA
(972) 497-9959

Fact and Fiction

This novel is a work of fiction, and the characters are entirely imagined by me, except for those who are specifically historical and bear their own names. While the book understandably reflects a few of my personal, travel, and professional experiences, it should not be considered autobiographical.

Keele Hall, St. John the Baptist Church at Keele, the University of Keele, High House, Lambeth Palace, Tree Tops Guest House (without the fictitious counseling service), and York Minster are real, as are many military details of the English Civil War included in this book. Other locations have basis in fact.

The fictional Mayfield family borrows the Sneade/Sneyd ancestral home at Keele and their coat of arms. The "Roundheads" (Parliamentarians) under Captain Barbour threatened the destruction of Keele Hall but looted only. The Sneade/Sneyd family history includes a secret marriage long ago at Keele. A special license to marry could only be obtained from an archbishop. Honour's romantic poesy ring, as well as coffin and skull mourning rings, were typical of the period. The massacre at Barthomley Church was

Circle of Love

an actual occurrence.

John Whitehead was Anglican vicar of St. John the Baptist Church at Keele during the novel's writing, rather than in the 1600's. W. Conroy actually served as curate there between 1636 and 1670.

The following persons are historical:

King Charles I and his nephew, Prince Rupert of the Rhine.

William Laud, the Archbishop of Canterbury, was imprisoned in the Tower of London, and later beheaded, during the English Civil War.

Sir Edmund Verney, King Charles' standard bearer at the Battle of Edgehill, perished there, and his widow received the news from Sir Edward Sydenham.

Samuel, Alice, and young son William Sneade immigrated in 1635 from England to Virginia on a land grant from King Charles I.

Richard Sneade/Sneyd owned High House at the time of King Charles' visit in mid-September 1642. Prince Rupert shot the tail of the church weathercock twice from High House on that visit.

Ralph Sneade/Sneyd, brother of Richard, was promoted to colonel by King Charles at High House.

William Comberford, local leader in Stafford, later became governor and an officer in the King's army.

Captain Barbour commanded the Parliament troops that marched on Keele Hall.

To Learn More

PROFESSIONAL VHS VIDEO DOCUMENTARY

A Visit to Keele: Home of the Sneyds, 26 minutes. NTSC (USA standard)

    Tour the setting of *Circle of Love*. See Keele Hall, built in 1580 and substantially rebuilt during the Victorian era, plus the Church of St. John the Baptist at Keele, and scenes of the University of Keele. Produced by Gary and Susan Bauer, with J.M. Kolbert as on-camera guide and historian. View demonstration footage on the Alpha Video website at www.alphavideo.net.
    Available for US$25 (check or money order payable to Alpha Video). Includes USA shipping and applicable sales tax. Contact:

        Alpha Video Productions
        1219 Abrams Road, Suite 316
        Richardson TX 75081 USA
        (972) 497-9959
        www.alphavideo.net
        alphagb@aol.com

THE INTERNATIONAL ASSOCIATION OF SNEEDS

A non-profit organization dedicated to preserving the genealogical records and family heritage of the Sneed/Sneyd/Sneade family in the U.S. and around the world. Reunions are held every two years. Newsletter subscriptions included in membership of $10 per year.

For membership information, contact:

> Martha Hirsch, Treasurer
> 9135 Arbor Glen Lane
> Charlotte NC 28210

For genealogical information, contact:

> Tom Sneed, Genealogist
> 15810 East Holdridge Road
> Wayzata MN 55391-2146
> Tsneed@wavefront.com

BOOKLETS ABOUT KEELE HALL AND THE SNEYDS BY J.M. KOLBERT

The Sneyds and Keele Hall, The University of Keele, 1967. US$4.00

The Sneyds: Squires of Keele, The University of Keele, 1976. US$6.00

Keele Hall: A Victorian Country House. Describes the rebuilding of Keele Hall in the mid-19th century. The University of Keele, 1986. Color photos.
ISBN 0 900770 68 6. US$8.50.

Set of all 3 booklets, combined price US$16.00. All prices include postage.

Order from from: D. Warrilow, Keele Information

Services, Keele University, Keele, Staffordshire ST5 5BG, England. Email orders: kis@keele.ac.uk. Questions: d.warrilow@lib.keele.ac.uk.

HISTORY OF THE UNIVERSITY OF KEELE BY J.M. KOLBERT

Keele, the first fifty years: A Portrait of the University 1950-2000, Keele: Melandrium Books, 2000, ISBN 1 85856 238 4.

Available from Melandrium Books, 11 Highway Lane, Keele ST5 5AN, Staffordshire, England. To mail order, send check or money order for US$35.00, including shipping. Credit card orders accepted on purchases through Trentham Books, Email: tb@trentham-books.co.uk.

THE ANCIENT HIGH HOUSE IN STAFFORD

This 400-year-old timber-framed townhouse was built in 1595 and is operated by the Stafford Borough Council. The Civil War Room exhibit includes wax figures of King Charles I and Prince Rupert visiting with Richard Sneade/Sneyd, while additional rooms represent other historical periods. There is also a military exhibit of the Staffordshire Yeomanry, the Queen's own royal regiment.

The High House is located on Greengate Street, Stafford ST16 2JA, England. Telephone +44 (0)1785 619 131. Fax +44 (0)1785 619 132. Normally open Monday through Saturday for tours. Free (as of December 2002). Gift shop. Please reconfirm the Ancient High House hours of operation before traveling to visit. Website: http://www.staffordbc.gov.uk. Email: ahh@staffordbc.gov.uk.

TREE TOPS GUEST HOUSE IN YORK

This lovely, family-operated bed and breakfast is conveniently located for touring York, and some rooms have views of York Minster. They can be contacted at 21 St. Mary's, Bootham, York YO30 7DD, England, phone/fax 01904 658053, Website: http://business.thisisyork.co.uk/treetops. Email: treetops.guesthouse@virgin.net.

Additional copies of *Circle of Love* are available from the following:

Credit card Internet sales:

www.XulonPress.com and other major bookseller websites.

Autographed or regular copies by check or money order for US $13.99 each, plus $3.99 shipping and handling:

>Attn: Susan Bauer
>Alpha Video Productions
>441 Biscay Drive
>Garland, TX 75043 USA
>(972) 497-9959
>www.alphavideo.net

(Please include check or money order payable to Alpha Video Productions. No credit card orders are available at this time through Alpha Video.)

Your favorite local bookstore can also order *Circle of Love* for you. Just refer to the ISBN on the back of this book.

Thank you.